THE BOY WHO LOVED ANNE FRANK

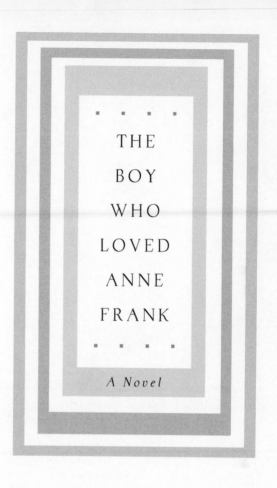

THE
BOY
WHO
LOVED
ANNE
FRANK

A Novel

Ellen Feldman

W. W. NORTON & COMPANY
NEW YORK   LONDON

For information about permission to reproduce selections from this book, write to
Permissions, W. W. Norton & Company, Inc., 500 Fifth Avenue, New York, NY 10110

Book design by Brian Mulligan

ISBN 0-7394-6033-1

W. W. Norton & Company, Inc., 500 Fifth Avenue, New York, N.Y. 10110

W. W. Norton & Company Ltd., Castle House, 75/76 Wells Street, London W1T 3QT

In memory of
Sina Baum
1917-1958

"He [Peter] said that after the war he'd make sure nobody would know he was Jewish."

—The Diary of a Young Girl,
by Anne Frank, February 16, 1944

"We have records of what happened to all the inhabitants of the secret annex except Peter."

—A guide on a tour of the
Anne Frank House, January 1994

PROLOGUE

August 13, 1946

■ ■ NOTHING SET HIM APART from the crowd, except the
■ ■ fact that he did not want to stand out. But you could
not tell that by looking at him. All you saw was a rawboned
young man with wolfish eyes, not unlike the mob of young
men shouldering one another in the aftermath of the war
and the huckster glare of neon signs and come-hither mar-
quees. You could tell he was an out-of-towner from the way
he was staring up at the rings of smoke rising from the
Camel sign above his head, but that did not make him spe-

cial. On a clement summer night, Times Square was full of tourists.

It had taken him a year to get here. That was how long it was, almost to the week, since he had seen that dog-eared copy of *Life* magazine with the photo of an American boy in a sailor suit, drunk on President Truman's announcement that the Japanese had surrendered, bending a white-uniformed nurse over backward in an orgasmic kiss of peace. As soon as he saw it, he knew where he was headed. Here was a country where uniforms were innocent as children's clothing. Here was a city where people could shout their joy to the rooftops. Here was a place where love would bend over backward to meet him.

The immaculate halos of American ingenuity continued to rise from the perfect O of the smoker's mouth. He knew how they worked, because he had struck up a friendship with a fellow on the ship's crew, whom he had pestered with questions all the way over. The rings were ten feet in diameter and not smoke but steam, collected from the building's heating system and stored in a reservoir behind the sign. Every four seconds, a piston-driven diaphragm forced the steam through the hole. What a country, what a people, to put their genius to such ends!

And now he was one of them. He had come down the gangplank onto the pier that morning an immigrant, a greenhorn, a displaced person. He had emerged from the customs shed an hour later, a one-hundred-percent American. And he had not even had to lie. All he had had to do was keep quiet. He had spent almost twenty-five months, seven hundred and fifty-three days to be exact, keeping quiet.

Shh. Don't talk. Don't move. Someone will hear.

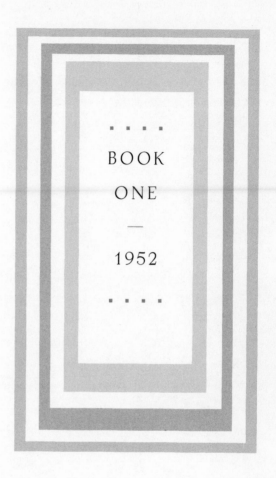

. . . .

BOOK

ONE

—

1952

. . . .

ONE

■ ■ THE DOCTOR'S NAME WAS GABOR. Like the Hungarian
■ ■ sisters with all the jewelry and all the husbands, I told
my wife. Zsa Zsa, Eva, and I always forget the third one. I was
trying to make a joke of it. I was trying to be a good sport. You
won't get anywhere with a chip on your shoulder, they had
warned me, though that had been years ago.

I had no chip on my shoulder now. I could not have been
more accommodating, as Dr. Gabor held open the door
between the waiting room and his office. He nodded his small
head, covered with an oil slick of gleaming black hair, for me
to go ahead of him. I stepped inside.

The slats of the Venetian blinds were clenched tight against the sun-fried afternoon. Shadows swallowed the corners of the room. Beneath the window, an air conditioner muttered unintelligible threats. Against one wall, a black leather chaise crouched. I gave it a wide berth and took the chair on the near side of the desk. Dr. Gabor made his way around it and sat in a larger chair across from me. He was not a big man, a head shorter than I and thirty pounds lighter, I would guess. I imagined his feet beneath the desk swinging several inches above the floor, at once jaunty and helpless. I could overwhelm him easily.

He reached for a yellow legal pad and plucked a pen from several stuck in an Etruscan vase. The desk was as cluttered as a pawnshop. There were the tricks of his trade: the paper and pen he had reached for, a telephone, half a dozen books with the spines turned toward him, a clock, also turned toward him. Then there were the curiosities, or perhaps they were just different tricks of the same trade: a reproduction of Rodin's *Burghers of Calais*—strange, in view of his profession, that he had not opted for *The Kiss*—several pre-Columbian heads with hollowed-out eyes and gaping mouths, two African statues, one with a distended stomach and breasts pendulous as eggplants, the other with a penis like a machine gun. Dr. Gabor had it trained on me. I wanted to tell him that was not the problem. There was a time when I was afraid it would be, but not anymore.

He leaned back in the chair and looked at me through wire-rimmed glasses. He had the wide, inane gaze of an owl. It was not reassuring. The other doctors had told me he was my last hope, this Hungarian gent in his nipped-in-the-waist double-breasted suit that hinted at long afternoons lost to boulevard cafés and languid hours with those blond creampuffs who shared his name. The suit could not be an accident. Clothes are the easiest camouflage. I was dressing like an American, or at least a GI, before I came down the gangplank that August morning. Perhaps that was the point. Dr. Gabor, who had been here for longer than I, since several years before the war according to the framed certificates on the wall, was advertising his connection to the Old World, or perhaps only resisting the vulgarities of the New. I was sure he would see them as vulgarities.

"So, Mr. van Pels," he said and rocked a little in his big leather chair, "you have lost your voice."

You have lost your mittens, you naughty kittens, my wife reads to our daughter.

I nodded, though these days I could whisper. For three weeks, I could not do even that. I could open my mouth, I could form the words, but I could not make a sound. Now I was capable of a pathetic mewl, weak as a baby's. No, a baby can howl. You should have heard my daughter roar when the doctor slapped her into life. Her cry reverberated around the world. I opened my own mouth to crow in celebration, but the sight of her, swinging by her mucus-slippery feet, raw and bloody as a piece of meat, stopped the cry in my throat. I imagined her sliding to the floor and splattering onto the patterned linoleum. I envisioned the doctor giving in to a giddy urge and my daughter sailing through the air and crashing against the bone-white wall. My wife doubts my memory of seeing our newborn daughter. She says I could not have been there. But she was sedated at the time, and I know I am not mistaken. Perhaps I was lurking just outside the delivery room and caught a glimpse when the door swung open. The sight of my daughter silenced me then, and something has stolen my voice now. No one can diagnose what it is.

I went to a battery of doctors. They stuck tubes down my throat, and x-rayed my neck, and pushed, and probed, and asked endless questions. I had to write the answers on a pad. What do you eat? Everything. How much do you drink? Not much. Do you smoke?

They all asked that, and I told them no. Did you ever smoke? They sounded like the Senate hearings I keep reading about in the papers. Are you now or have you ever been? Never, I wrote, though I had tried cigarettes occasionally as a boy. I still like the aroma. For some reason I find it soothing. But the vicarious pleasure is sufficient. I never acquired the habit. I did not tell them all that. There was enough to write without the unimportant details.

They moved on to the allergies. Are you allergic to anything? Not that I know of, I wrote on the pad. What about as a boy? Any record of childhood allergies? No, I scribbled. No record of childhood allergies. No record of childhood. It was confiscated, burned, bombed out of existence. It was hidden away in a secret place, so secret I cannot remember it. I did not write that either.

"Was the loss gradual?" Dr. Gabor asked me now. "Did it happen suddenly, or did you feel your voice getting weaker?"

"Overnight," I croaked. "Literally. I went to sleep with a voice, and got up without one."

"Did anything unusual happen during the night?"

I shook my head no.

"What about dreams?"

"I do not dream."

He went on staring at me.

"I do not," I repeated.

He leaned farther back in his chair and looked at me over a long narrow nose that bisected a face flat as the Great Hungarian Plain. "Tell me about yourself, Mr. van Pels."

"I am a builder by profession," I whispered. "I have a wife and two daughters, three and eighteen months. I live in Indian Hills. That is our development, my partner's and mine."

Gabor looked up from the pad.

"That is all," I rasped.

"Where were you born? I detect a slight accent."

You detect a slight accent, Doctor? You, with that singsong speech like the Hungarian flag waving in the wind. I have yet to meet one of your countrymen who can rid himself of the cadence. My accent gives away less. Not exactly German, people begin when they are trying to identify me. A hint of Dutch, they guess. You learned British English, not American, my wife remarked the first time I spoke to her. She says she fell in love with my French accent, though I tell her it is not as good as she thinks.

I may be better at French, Peter, but you're much better at English.

"Osnabrück," I whispered.

"So you're German."

"I am an American citizen."

"German by birth, I mean."

"My father was Dutch. So was his father. I just happen to have been born in Germany."

"That was when?"

"November eighth, 1926," I told him, though August 13, 1946, would have been closer to the truth.

"And you arrived here?"

"August thirteenth, 1946."

"So you were in Germany during the war?"

No one will know we're here. You can't even see it from outside.

"I was in Europe."

"Are you Jewish, Mr. van Pels?"

"Are you, Doctor?"

"I am not important. Merely a tool to help us understand you."

"There is nothing to understand."

"To understand why you lost your voice. You said you were born in Germany, but were elsewhere in Europe during the war. That was why I asked if you were Jewish."

"No. But my wife is."

I do not usually tell people that, but if we were going to talk about what I had been up to in Europe during the war, it seemed like a good idea. It might also prevent awkwardness somewhere down the line. A few months ago, the fellow I deal with over at First Mutual asked if I was interested in joining the country club, then never mentioned it again. I would not have joined in any event, but the fact that since then he has not been able to meet my eyes when the subject of golf comes up is bad for business.

"Then you were in the army? You would have been . . ."—he glanced down at the yellow pad—"thirteen when the war began, eighteen by the end."

"I spent most of the war in Amsterdam."

I could see him thinking as he wrote. What were you doing in Amsterdam, Mr. van Pels? Rounding up Jews, since you are not one of the chosen people, or just beating the hell out of

Dutch citizens? He was not the only one who wondered. As far as I could see, the suspicions were the only drawback to not being a Jew. Who, given the recent history of the world, would have thought there were any?

"What about your family? Did they come to this country with you?"

The American Consulate

Rotterdam

This is to certify that as of February 10, 1939, Hermann, Auguste, and Peter van Pels have been placed on the waiting list for emigration to America.

"My parents are dead."

He went on staring at me.

"War casualties." The word was a sibilant whisper in the gloomy office.

"Sisters or brothers?"

It will be like having two sisters.

It will be like having two girlfriends—on the premises. Look at him blush, Kerli.

"No brothers or sisters."

"Any surviving relatives?"

Did he want a list? Grandpa Aaron arrested after Kristallnacht, dead before we went into hiding; Aunt Hetty at Auschwitz, Aunt Klara at Sobibor.

I shook my head no.

"I'm sorry," he murmured, and I could see him reconsidering. Whatever I had been up to during the war, and he was still wondering about that, it had not been all beer and skittles. Convenient, those Britishisms. From the beginning, they set me apart from the other displaced persons and greenhorns, greenies, as those who had been here a generation, or even a decade, called us.

"It must have been difficult," he went on.

Difficult. Ah, the words we come up with to keep the unthinkable at bay. Yes, Doctor, it was difficult. But also, shame to say, useful. If I had not been alone, I might not be sitting here now. I knew a fellow in the DP camp, a Pole, who did not lose his entire family in the blink of an eye or even over the course of a year. His wife survived, and three of his five children. Come to think of it, I knew him before the DP camp, when he thought he had lost them all. We were living on the outside then, surviving off the land, taking what we needed where we could.

Enough, Peter. We've had enough fun for one night. Besides, the old man has nothing. He sleeps in the barn with his animals.

But then he learned that his wife and three of his children had survived. In the DP camp they had another baby. The rush to replace in that camp was something to behold. I understood it, but I also knew the facts of life. I was not going to repeat my father's mistake at the American Consulate in Rotterdam. A young healthy man without dependents stood the best chance of getting a visa. Add a wife and you went down a few notches. Add four children, and you might as well abandon hope. But the Pole was an operator. He managed to qualify, despite the wife and four children. He managed to get the whole family as far as the medical exam. That was the one thing no one could finesse. And that was when they found the spots on his wife's lungs. I could not imagine why they were surprised. The real shock was that everyone in the camp did not have lung spots or tuberculosis or a dozen other diseases and deficiencies. My body was harboring its own memento of those years when I had been locked away in an attic like a discarded souvenir, living on rotten potatoes and moldy beans, though I did not know it at the time. But the Pole's wife had spots. She told him to go without her. Once the spots cleared up, she would follow with the children. He said, no dice. He had been perfecting his American slang for months. No dice, they would go as a family or not at all. Not at all was the outcome. While they were waiting for the spots to disappear, the authorities closed down the camp and repatriated everybody. Then Uncle Joe Stalin dropped his curtain, and now the Pole and his wife and four children were stuck in a communist sinkhole, if they were alive. So you see, Dr. Gabor, there were advantages to having no one, though it does not do to say so.

"What about in this country? Did you have any relatives when you arrived?"

He had signed the sponsorship papers and sent the money, but he had not asked when I was arriving, and I had not written to tell him. I could barely remember my father's brother, the one who had stood higher on the list at the American Consulate in Rotterdam. Uncle was one more word without a meaning.

I shook my head no.

"It must have been difficult." He repeated the all-purpose word for a world beyond his imagination, but this time he was wrong. Before America was difficult, if you had to attach a palliative to it. America was, in fact, beer and skittles.

"I was happy to be here."

"Tell me about it."

Where would I begin, Doctor? That first morning on the

pier? I do not think so. I have not told even my wife about that. Or should I try to explain the unlikely one-in-a-million meeting after it, when I thought the game was up before it had even begun?

"Amsterdam," the man outside the pier said when he saw the tag on my suitcase. "Perhaps you knew my father."

We were American residents now, free to go where we wanted, but still we clung together out of fear, or habit, or suspicion. At least they did. I was in a hurry to get away. But he had planted himself in front of me, this remnant of my past, though I did not know that at the time. I had heard of him, but we had never met, and standing face to face on the pier, I thought he was just another refugee. All over Europe, people were stumbling through barbed wire, across whole countries, back to bombed-out neighborhoods, asking again and again. You were in such-and-such camp; did you know so-and-so? Have you any word of this one? Any news of that one? They studied Red Cross lists, and placed ads in newspapers, and plagued anyone who would give them the time of day. And the longer they asked the questions, the more terrified they became of the answers.

"Perhaps you knew my father," the man repeated, though he must have seen that I was trying to get away from him. "Fritz Pfeffer. He was a dentist in Amsterdam."

So this was Werner, the son just a year younger than I, whom Pfeffer had had the sense to get out on a kindertransport to England right after Kristallnacht. I had come halfway around the world to run into the boy I had spent two years envying. I owed him nothing, not even information. I suggested he check with the Red Cross.

"I already did that. My father died in Neuengamme. I'm looking for people who knew him while he was alive. After I left." He dropped his eyes for a moment, but I would not pity him. He had spent the war in England. "I heard he went into hiding with a family called Frank," he said.

I told him I knew nothing of a dentist named Pfeffer or a family called Frank. The truth would have given him no solace. You probably do not agree, Doctor, but you are not in a position to judge. You do not know the spitefulness of memories.

"There is nothing to tell," I said to the doctor now. "I came by ship. It docked in New York. I was, as I said, happy to be here."

"Where did you live when you first arrived? With a family? At a facility?"

Facility. Another anodyne word, but what else could you call the Marseilles? It was no longer a hotel, despite the carved letters on the façade, only a way station on the grand tour of misery; a noisy, crumbling layover for old people of forty or fifty, who would never learn to speak English because they were afraid of the stories they could tell; and children who trembled when they had to get in line for the dining room or the doctor or the showers; and men and girls with wary eyes and brittle smiles and a ready answer for every question, a dozen answers, just tell me which you want to hear. One girl, who had long blond hair she kept running her fingers through, as if to make sure it was still there, used to give me smiles as thin as the new dimes in my pocket when we passed in the hall. I smiled back, but I always kept going.

Or should I tell you about the Marseilles tango, Doctor? How could I describe that sorry dance of desperation to someone like you, with your wall of credentials that would make you an upright, first-rate pillar of any community? Even if you had seen the dance, you would not have understood the steps.

They stood in front of the map. THIS IS WHAT AMERICA LOOKS LIKE was written in infantilely large letters above it. A man or woman or child would point to a spot. The gesture was blind and haphazard, as if they were playing a children's party game. The other dancers—a wife, a father, an aged aunt who had a few drops of the same blood pumping from her broken heart—would follow the advancing finger and come to rest on a dot. Greensboro. Cleveland. Detroit. Then one of them would take the red or white or blue ribbon attached to the spot between thumb and forefinger and follow it to the corresponding picture stuck on the wall around the map. That was when the arguments began. Like all tangos, the one they danced in the Marseilles lobby was charged with passion.

"It looks too much like Lodz."

"What are you talking, it doesn't look enough like Lodz."

"There's too much snow. We'll freeze to death."

"Look at those palm trees. A jungle they're sending us to."

They slid back and forth, pointing at the map, peering at the pictures, reading omens in the familiarity of a gothic façade, the dulcet sound of a street name, the contented gaze of a crowd of strangers, until a violinist who had played in a string quartet in Budapest decided the home of the Philadelphia Orchestra could not be such a terrible place, and a woman who had never been outside a small village in Romania finally believed the social worker who promised her there were no Indians in Indianapolis. I knew I had to get out of there, and not by way of the tango.

"I found a room," I told the doctor.

Everyone had said it was impossible. Had I not heard there was a housing shortage? All over the country people were living in old army barracks and cars and other people's porches. One couple had taken up residence in a department store window in hope someone would take notice and rent them a flat. But I managed to find a room, a tunnel really, with a single window in front that was on a level with the sidewalk. It cost nine dollars a month, and I was lucky to get it. I did not even mind the subterranean view. Late at night or early in the morning, I lay in bed and watched the feet go by. Occasionally, a pair of high heels with open toes passed. The painted nails winked, and my imagination sent up a gale-force wind that sucked the oblivious wearer of those not-so-innocent shoes, hair blowing, clothes flying off, through the window and into my narrow iron bed.

"I found a job. First as a waiter. When I got a driver's license, I drove a taxi too."

"Very impressive," Dr. Gabor said, but he could not resist glancing at the diplomas and certificates that papered his walls, as if to make sure they were still there.

I did not bother to tell him there was nothing impressive about it. We all held down more than one job. Some went to night school as well, but I did not have the patience for that. I could not even sit still to read. I tried. I went to the library and took out books. In that cramped fetid hideaway, books had been our escape. We worked our way through Goethe and Schiller and Dickens and Thackeray. But in America I no longer needed an escape. Who would want to escape from the Promised Land? A page or two into those library books, I would toss them aside, and grab my hat and coat, and pound up the three steps from my basement room to the real world that was right outside my door, and suddenly within my reach.

I prowled Fulton Street and Borough Hall and Grand Army Plaza, walked the Brooklyn Bridge, loped up Broadway and down Park Avenue, and crossed from the East River to the Hudson and back again. I lingered in Prospect and Riverside and Central Parks to spy on young mothers with toddlers and nurses with big English prams, stopped on the street to watch boys play stickball, and followed, at discreet distances, elegantly dressed women up Fifth Avenue and down Madison. Once I climbed to the top of a double-decker bus, because I had read in the paper they were being replaced by single-deckers, but I was in too much of a hurry for the traffic jams and the long stops while passengers shuffled off and on and fished in their pockets for coins. If I was going to ride, I preferred the El. I liked the speed, and the secret glimpses into other people's lives. I sat in the jaundiced-lit cars and peered into the windows of Harlem tenements crowded with children, and Tudor City apartments where women stood over stoves while men sat reading evening papers, and Brooklyn brownstones where entire families went about their individual but attached lives in a checkerboard of illuminated squares. Sometimes I sat in the El as it shrieked and clattered and careened around corners and wanted to open my mouth and let out the emptiness in a long piercing howl. But even that was better than reading. I had no patience with stories that were not real or information that I could not use immediately.

The movies were another story. At the movies I could perfect my English. Once, a woman in front of me called the usher because I was making too much noise murmuring the dialogue a split second after the actors, but usually I managed to repeat the words under my breath. And at the movies I was less lonely. The darkness hummed with the nearness of other bodies. The stars were old friends.

I have other photos of movie stars, Peter, if you'd like more to hang over your bed.

"And now you build houses," Dr. Gabor said. "That's quite a success story."

I knew what he was thinking. How had a greenie like me got to a place like this? But I had not taken advantage of Harry. The idea was mine, but Harry went for it. No one had to twist his arm.

"Tell me about your wife, Mr. van Pels."

Tell me, tell me, he kept insisting. Could the man not hear I had no voice?

"Did you meet here or in Europe?"

If you saw her teeth, Doctor, you would not ask that. They are a testament to a lifetime of pasteurized milk, and fresh vegetables, and expensive dental care. The first time she smiled at me, I was dazzled. The same with her sister.

"I met her here. She was born here."

"And you say she's Jewish?"

The time will come when we'll be people again and not just Jews!

I nodded.

"Is that a source of friction between you?"

He was on to something there, but the friction was not between us, it was within me. I had never intended to marry a Jew, I was dead set against it, but a man cannot help where he falls in love.

"I married her."

"So you were attracted to the fact that she was Jewish?"

Attracted! It was love at first sight, but not because she was Jewish. I was besotted, with her, with her sister, with her father, who could barely hide his pleasure at having another man at the table that first night I began insinuating myself into the bosom of the family, with her mother, who did not quite trust me. A shrewd woman, my mother-in-law.

"I am sorry, Doctor, but I do not see where this is getting us. I lost my voice. There are no other problems in my life." I leaned forward and tapped his desk with my knuckles. I meant it as a joke. I am not a superstitious man.

"Have you ever had an incident of this sort in the past?" he asked.

"I never lost my voice," I whispered.

"Any other health problems that did not seem to have a physiological origin?"

"You mean any psychosomatic illnesses?"

He shrugged his padded linen shoulders.

"Shortly after I got here, I developed a tremor in my hands and legs. The first doctor I went to told me I had a case of institutionitis."

"Pardon me?"

Certainly, Doctor. I do not blame you. The man was a fool, but I went to him because he had a reputation. Everyone at the Marseilles knew how much he hated Europe. The graveyard of the Jews, he called it. A man like that was not likely to send anyone, even a gentile, back. That was my greatest fear. If they could keep you out of the country for illness, could they deport you for the same reason? I would not be betrayed by my own body.

They'll hear the coughing.

Give him more codeine.

Do you want to kill him?

If the workers downstairs hear that coughing, we're all dead.

The possibility had kept me from consulting a doctor for weeks. I lay in bed, the iron frame knocking against the wall from my trembling, my fear-fogged mind hallucinating other rank-smelling rooms. Finally I had no choice. I went to the doctor who hated Europe.

"He said I was afraid to be on my own and wanted to go back to the DP camp," I told Dr. Gabor. "I spent several months in a camp before I got my visa. He said I wanted people to take care of me. Institutionitis."

That was how I knew the tremors were not psychosomatic. The last thing I wanted was to be at the mercy of others.

"Did the tremors disappear, or do you still suffer from them?"

"They disappeared. After I went to another doctor. It turned out I had an overactive thyroid."

Dr. Gabor made another note, then put down his pen and leaned back in the chair again. "Tell me about the night you lost your voice, Mr. van Pels. Do you remember anything remarkable about it?"

I shook my head no.

"What did you do that night?"

"I drove home from the office, I played with my daughters, my wife and I had dinner, we read the paper and watched television, we went to bed. It was just like any other night."

"The sexual side of your marriage is satisfactory?"

"Absolutely."

"You make love how often, once a month, once a week, more than that?"

"More," I whispered.

"Did you make love that night? The night you lost your voice?"

I looked at the African statue he had trained on me. I nodded.

"And you had a satisfactory climax? No dysfunction?"

A whiff of debauchery wafted across his desk.

"No dysfunction," I mumbled.

"What about your wife? Did she have an orgasm?"

My wife, Doctor, is none of your goddamn business. Not the suction-cup sweetness of her mouth, or the arched-back exuberance of her seat, as we would call it if she were riding a horse, or the eerie wail that always reminds me of the final notes from Bunny Berigan's trumpet at the end of "I Can't Get Started." She played that song the night she took me out to mend my broken heart. I can still see her feeding coins into the fat, flashing, all-American jukebox. Sometimes, when that sound escapes from her now, I wonder if she knew, in her restless virginity, that was the noise she would make, if she played it for me in promise of things to come. I wonder, Doctor, but it is none of your fucking business.

I nodded again, and kept my hand, which was balled into a fist, behind me.

"And afterward? Was there any disagreement or recrimination?"

"Whatever is wrong with my voice," I whispered, "has nothing to do with sex."

"I'm just trying to find out what happened that evening. Did you talk? Did you go to sleep?"

"I went to sleep."

"And your wife?"

The Burghers of Calais glowed dully in the dim light. It must have weighed a good ten pounds. The raised arm of Pierre de Wissant could put out a man's eye.

"She read. She always reads before she falls asleep."

"Does that bother you?"

"Her reading?"

"Her reading after you make love?"

"Why should it?"

"Some people might perceive it as emotional abandonment."

You call lying in hot sheets that smell of sex and sweat and laundry soap, nerves humming, children dreaming in the next room, flank covered, abandonment? Perhaps you have chosen the wrong profession, Doctor. Or perhaps you have spent too much time in those boulevard cafés.

"It does not bother me."

"What was your wife reading that night?"

The question was absurd, but they said he was my only hope. I tried to picture my wife sitting up in bed, taking the book from the night table, settling back into the pillows. I tried to see the volume propped on the blue satin border of the electric blanket. It was not one of the fat, finger-worn paper-bound books from her college days that she sometimes brought to bed. *Madame Bovary. Anna Karenina.* Thackeray's book about the colonel. I knew that one well. We read it the second spring we spent in hiding. The book she was reading that night was new, fresh off the bookstore shelves or out of its cardboard Book-of-the-Month Club wrapper. I narrowed my eyes to bring the slick jacket into focus. Bold black letters. A photograph.

"Are you all right?" Gabor asked.

"What?"

"You just grabbed hold of the chair, as if you were going to fall."

I told him he was mistaken. I was merely shifting position.

"We were talking about what your wife was reading the night you lost your voice."

"Just a book."

"You don't remember what it was?"

"Does it matter?"

For the first time Gabor smiled. "Probably not. I was merely curious about her taste."

"She reads everything. But I did not notice what she was reading that night."

"There is no point in wasting away in mourning, no point in brooding. We have to go on living, go on building."

—Otto Frank in letter to his brother, March 16, 1946, quoted in *The Hidden Life of Otto Frank* by Carol Ann Lee

T W O

■ ■ I CAME OUT OF DR. GABOR'S building, a squat poured-
■ ■ concrete lair of professional offices, into a wall of heat. It thickened the air and turned the parking lot soft beneath my shoes. As I crossed to the car, I slipped out of my jacket and pulled off my tie, but left my shirtsleeves buttoned. It is not that I am ashamed. I just see no reason to flaunt it.

"What's that, Daddy?" my older daughter asks, her small hand hovering over it, afraid to touch it, dying to put her finger on the spot.

"Just something Daddy got when he was little," I say, and the answer deflects her. She does not want to think of me as any smaller than I am. She needs all the height and bulk and substance she can get. She is no fool, my daughter.

I had left the windows open, but the inside of the car was still suffocating. The leather seat burned through my shirt. The steering wheel stuck to my hands. Only the key that had been in my pocket during the time I had spent in Dr. Gabor's office was not hot to the touch.

I turned the ignition and reached for the radio knob. The metal scalded my fingers. Even the announcer's voice was overheated, but then I was still tuned in my head to the BBC broadcasters. They had been unflappable. The Americans were merely smug. Five hundred U.N. planes had bombed North Korea. The House had repassed the immigration bill, or rather the anti-immigration bill, over President Truman's veto. Ninety-seven degrees and no relief in sight.

I pulled into the stream of traffic crawling along Route One. Was there anything remarkable about that night? the doctor had asked. Everything, Doctor, everything that evening, and the one before it, and the one after it, and tonight. The shards of sunlight splintering off the hood of the car like diamonds; the signs throbbing in the heat promising me 26 CENTS A GALLON, and TWO-FOR-ONE, and PARKING IN THE REAR; the scowling driver who swerves heedlessly in front of me and the one who waves me ahead with a gesture of noblesse oblige; the towering shade trees along the sun-dappled access road and the heady smell of fresh-cut grass as I get closer to home. It is all remarkable, Doctor, and how strange that after everything, it can still break my heart. Or maybe that is the point.

I turned onto Indian Hills Road. My left foot came down on the brake, as my right foot eased up on the gas. It is a peculiar habit, though I did not know it until my wife pointed it out. She was not my wife then.

"You drive with both feet," she said in the same tone of fascination she remarked on the number of languages I spoke or the books I had read before I stopped reading.

"What do you mean?"

"Most people move one foot from the gas pedal to the brake. You keep one foot on each."

I looked down at the floor of the car. Sure enough, I had one polished brown shoe resting on each pedal.

"Did you ever have the feeling that you wanted to go and still have the feeling that you wanted to stay?" she sang in a parody of Jimmy Durante. She had been surprised too by my familiarity with American entertainers and movie stars.

"It's a sign of ambivalence," she said about my feet.

"It's the way I drive," I told her, though for a while after that I tried to use one foot, the way she said everyone else did. But after a week or two, I reverted to my old habits. I felt safer that way.

I was driving with both feet now, and both hands on the wheel. The speedometer needle trembled between twenty-five and thirty. My partner Harry says if he were ever going to buy a used car, which God forbid he should have to, he would buy it from me. Either me or the little old lady who used it only to drive to church on Sundays, he adds, because he wants me to know he is just teasing. Harry can joke all he wants, but what he does not understand is how easily accidents happen. Even here. Especially here, where sprinklers fling rainbows across newly seeded yards, and Windexed picture windows make everyone's life an open book, and children pedal bikes, not the black bicycles of burden that swarmed the streets of Amsterdam until the Germans took those away too, but bikes the colors of the stones in the jewelry my mother-in-law exacts in loving tribute from my father-in-law, who, like many businessmen, did well during the war. The children on the bicycles are my worst fear. I imagine them bouncing off the waxed hood of my Buick. I see them slipping under the whitewall tires.

I turned the car from Algonquin onto Iroquois. The move was instinctive. I could have found my way home with my eyes closed, were it not for fear of hitting those children. Sometimes when I drive these roads, I picture the view from above. I look down and see the ranches and Cape Cods and Colonials laid out on the curving streets, attached to the access road, connected to the highway, appended to the township, in the county of Middlesex, in the state of New Jersey, in the country of the United States of America. And I see myself, both feet on the pedals, both hands on the wheel, driving through it. I see, as Dr. Gabor could not when he asked all those niggling questions about sex, the forest for the trees.

As I turned right onto Seminole, I felt the familiar flash of panic. The house would not be there. In its place would be smoking ruins. Worse than that, in its place would be an untroubled expanse of grass and trees. No house ever existed. I had dreamed it. And in a moment I would wake up and be back in that other world. But the house was there. I exhaled and turned into the driveway.

A blur of blue and white loomed in my peripheral vision. My left foot came down on the brake. I did not stop short, I merely slowed a little. I turned my head to see what had caught my eye. Scottie Wiener, face scrubbed, wet hair slicked to his head, wearing a pair of blue-and-white-striped pajamas that were a couple of sizes too big, was standing in his yard. He was some distance from the driveway. I would have had to make a concerted effort to run him down.

I waved, and Scottie waved back. "Hi, Mr. van Peth," he called through the gap in his teeth. The neighborhood children like me. I am patient with them. I do not raise my voice, as some of the fathers do. I never lose my temper. At least, they have never seen me do so. A few weeks ago, I let Scottie help me put up the swing set in our backyard.

I turned away from the skinny, gap-toothed boy, trans-formed into a shriveled old man by his older brother's over-sized striped pajamas, and eased the car into the garage, careful to clear the station wagon, which my wife had pulled far to the side to leave room for me. The lawnmower and rakes and shovels and other tools for keeping chaos at bay were neatly stowed and hung.

I climbed out of the front seat, reached back in to get my tie and jacket, and sidled between the two cars to the back door. Ten days of record heat had swelled the wood, and I had to push with my shoulder to open it. The house was well made, for a tract model, and I had fixed everything I could, but it would never be as solid as I wanted.

The wall of cool air hit me as hard as the heat had when I came out of Dr. Gabor's office. I had put one air-conditioning unit in the family room and another in our bedroom. I pushed the door shut behind me, opened my mouth, remembered my voice, and closed it again. Then, because I could not resist, I mouthed the words, "I'm home."

Home. It is one of my favorite English words. The round full *o*; the plummy *m*. It is more solid than the slippery *house,* better than the sibilant *safe,* which is a fairy tale in any event. The only safe I trust is the one I installed with my own hands in the back of the linen closet when we moved into the house. Home, however, is a horse, or a word, of a different color.

I started across the family room. The playpen in the middle took up a lot of space, but there was still plenty of area around it. The room was larger than its counterparts in Pineview or Devon or any of the other developments in the vicinity. That was my idea. My brainstorm, Harry still calls it, though the concept was so simple I could not believe someone had not come up with it before me.

As I crossed the room, the ash-gray face of the television threw back my reflection. A tall man with short hair and a seersucker jacket hooked over his shoulder on one finger, a husband, a father, a businessman, an American. I ticked them off the way another man might pat his pockets to make sure he had his wallet and keys and lighter, if he smoked, which I do not.

I climbed the five stairs to the kitchen. A copy of *The Joy of Cooking,* stained with the expectations and ingredients of a couple of hundred dinners, lay open on the counter. The highchair in the corner was smeared with the strained and pureed aftermath of a struggle. At one end of the Formica table, macaroni and cheese congealed on a plate. It must have been a difficult supper. My wife usually scrapes the children's leftovers into the trash before I get home. Maybe it was the sight of them, or maybe it was Dr. Gabor, but suddenly I was back at the Marseilles. Never, not even before the war, had I seen so much food. Vats of soup and troughs of salad, steam tables of meat and fish and chicken and vegetables, and multitiered skyscrapers supporting plates of trembling jewel-colored pies and whipped-cream-crested cakes. There was as much food as I wanted, so much that I almost believed someday there might be enough. In the short time I stayed at the Marseilles, I became a legend. "Here he comes," the chesty pouter pigeon volunteers, corseted into their dark dresses, murmured to one another as I made my way down the line with my metal tray, "the trencherman." On the other side of the steam tables, their sweat-and-rouge-streaked faces stretched into man-eating grins as they competed to fill my plate. And I let them. I was practically doing them a favor.

I picked up my daughter's half-empty glass of milk and drained it. Even my request that first night at the Marseilles had not tarnished my reputation. "A glass of milk he wants, with meat." They shook their heads and clicked their tongues in mock horror. "Don't you know anything?" A tiny woman with sparse white hair, standing behind me in line, spoke up. "So he eats meat with milk. So he's traife." She raised her watery eyes to the ceiling and shook a child-tiny fist at heaven. The number on her arm flashed in the overhead light. "So do him something. You ain't done enough already, do him some-thing for this." The women behind the troughs of food dropped their eyes. The diminutive fury unclenched her fist and carried her tray to a table, as if she had not said a word.

I took my daughter's glass and plate to the sink and stood look-ing out the window as I ran water into them. The mimosa trees I had planted the year before were thriving. My wife had wanted a chestnut tree, but something in me did not like the idea of look-ing out the window at a chestnut tree. I did not tell her that. What kind of a man has a prejudice against chestnut trees? I merely hinted darkly at chestnut blight and said mimosas would be more exotic. My wife likes the unusual. I am living proof of that.

A narrow ribbon of woods separates Indian Hills from the golf course of the country club, the one the fellow at First Mutual talked to me about joining, until he found out my wife was Jewish. The woods and the golf course are selling points, but the view I prefer is of my neighbors' houses, or rather into their houses. No one draws blinds or closes curtains in the kitchens and living and family rooms of Indian Hills. Upstairs privacy is permitted, but downstairs demands full disclosure. My wife says it makes her uneasy to look out the window and see a neighbor in a mirror-image kitchen chopping onions or scrambling eggs or washing dishes just as she is. But I love to stand in my own house looking into theirs, seeing the simple greed smeared on their faces as they chew their bloody steaks and swallow their flash-frozen vegetables, and the complacency of their unguarded expressions as they sprawl in front of their televisions, and the breathtaking innocence of their hugs and kisses as they hustle their children off to sleep, certain they will be there the next morning.

As I stood looking out the window of my kitchen, Jane Wiener appeared in the window of hers. She was standing at the counter, her head bent, her childishly thin shoulders moving as she worked. She lifted one arm to push the straight black hair back from her forehead and stared out into the yard with her huge dark eyes. Suddenly her delicately boned face creased into a smile at some private joke or happiness, and I imagined, though I could not see them at this distance, the dimples.

Why do you always want me to smile?

Because you get dimples in your cheeks.

I am fond of Jane, though I know her no better than any of the other wives on the street, which is to say not well. But for some reason, I feel an attachment to her.

I turned off the water, crossed the room, and climbed another short flight to the upstairs hall. As I got closer, the sound of shrieks and giggles and a woman's voice crooning, "My ship has sails that are made of silk," slightly off-key grew louder. "What kind of a mother sings Kurt Weill to babies?" my mother-in-law asks. What kind of a girl marries a greenie she knows nothing about, a stranger who could be a thief or a murderer or a Nazi, despite that number on his arm, because we all know what some did to survive, is what she means. My mother-in-law has no idea what some did to survive, but that is beside the point. She is on to something about me.

I opened the door to the bathroom. My wife was on her knees, bending over the side of the tub with her back to the door and the pale soles of her feet exposed to the world. How can she walk around like that, presenting a vulnerable surface to broken glass and rusty nails and a hundred hidden booby traps? My eye moved up her body from those narrow dancer-arched invitations to trouble to the purple shorts that turned her behind into a ripe plum. My hand curled to the shape.

Beyond her, two small soap-slick, sun-browned bodies splashed deliriously. My older daughter stood to reach for me, slipped, and disappeared beneath the rim of the tub. I lunged. My wife's arm, brown and soap-slicked as the girls' bodies, reached in and pulled Abigail back into view, her hair streaming, her mouth open wide to let out the peals of laughter.

"Dad-dy, dad-dy, dad-dy!" Betsy shrieked like a siren. No, like the all-clear signal.

My wife turned toward the door. The heat and humidity had fashioned her dark hair into an unruly cloud. She flashed the milk-fed smile at me.

This, Dr. Gabor, is the definition of remarkable.

"TELL ME about the doctor," my wife said.

I was carrying the dinner dishes from the table to the kitchen counter, while she went through the familiar routine. Swab, rinse, stoop, swab, rinse, stoop. She was washing the dishes before she put them in the machine designed to wash them, just as all the wives up and down these wide winding streets did. Usually I tease her about it, as all the husbands tease their wives, and the ordinariness of the exchange always pleases me, but I did not tease her tonight, because I knew how much it had cost her to wait this long to ask about Dr. Gabor.

That morning she had assured me she respected the confidentiality of the therapeutic relationship. My wife took several psychology courses at Barnard College, though, unlike her sister, she did not major in the subject. But she had gleaned enough to worry. She feared what the doctor might discover was wrong with me. She fretted about what he might lead me to decide was wrong with her. So she could not help asking about him, despite her respect for the therapeutic relationship, and the fact that marriage to me had got her out of the habit of inquiring too closely into things.

"He asked a lot of questions."

"About what?"

"Everything. Me. You."

She turned from the sink and stood facing me. She had

washed her face and brushed her hair, but she had not put on any makeup. Her skin was brown from afternoons in the yard with the children. Her long eyes, hazel flecked with green lights and too much trust for her own good, narrowed with concern. "What about me?"

"You don't have to whisper," I said. "You have not lost your voice."

She turned back to the dishwasher.

I had not intended to sound irritable, but I did not like talking about Dr. Gabor. It was almost as bad as talking to him. Fifteen dollars an hour to discuss what books my wife was reading.

"He also wanted to know about my family. About before."

She went on standing with her back to me. Those were the questions she wanted to ask. "Tell me," she used to say in the beginning, "I want to know."

She did not want to know, but that was one more thing I did not tell her.

"And about sex."

"I thought he would." She turned to me again, and her long upper lip grew longer as her front teeth worried her lower lip. She distrusted her lack of experience. I never told her how grateful I had been for it.

"I explained to him that whatever was wrong with my voice had nothing to do with that."

"What does he think it has to do with?"

"He has no idea. That was why he asked all those questions. He even wanted to know what you read."

I had not meant to bring that up, though I had been unable to keep from stopping at the table on her side of the bed when

I went upstairs before dinner. But I had lost my voice weeks ago. She had probably read half a dozen books since then. *The Devil's Advocate* by Taylor Caldwell lay on the table now.

"What a funny thing to ask."

"It was a fishing expedition. He has no idea what he is after."

"Whatever you can remember. It's free association."

As I said, she had taken a few courses.

"But I cannot remember."

It was not a lie. There are things I could tell her, and choose not to. But there are other things I am not sure of. I have no trouble with the recent past. I never forget her birthday, or our anniversary, or the moment I knew I was going to marry her, which, she insists, was almost a year after she made up her mind to marry me. I can recall the weights of my daughters at birth, and the days I brought them home from the hospital, and that first night I spent sitting beside Abigail's crib. I am capable of coming out of a meeting at the office and repeating everything that was said and who said it, can tell you the costs of materials last year and the year before that, and carry specifications around in my head. On my current life, I am an authority. But my existence before is a mystery. Even when I try to remember it, I have difficulty. But sometime when I am not trying, when I am playing with the children, or sitting in my office, or thinking about matters that have nothing to do with the past, an explosion goes off, like the bombs from the Allied planes coming in high over the Westertoren steeple, and I glimpse the world the way I used to during those air raids, sharp and white and blinding. I even hear the sirens and smell the fires. A few months ago we had a fire on the site, and Harry kept complaining about the stench, but you do not know what fire smells like until you have inhaled a burning city. That is how vivid those flashes of memory are. But before I can get hold of them, the world goes dark again, just as it used to during the bombing raids. I know certain facts about my life. I can even put them together in sequence, because that must be the way they occurred. But I have no recollection of when things happened, or where they happened, or even if they happened to me or someone else. I was born six years ago in a customs shed on the Hudson River. I was conceived a year before that on a lightning-charged night in a dung-smelling barn somewhere in Germany. Any previous existence is a rumor I overheard. Instead of memory, I have instincts; in place of a past, I have this inexplicable, ill-gotten, entirely remarkable present.

"Others believe that the Displaced Person is a
human being, which he is not, and this applies par-
ticularly to the Jews who are lower than animals . . .
a subhuman species without any of the cultural or
social refinements of our time."
                                    —General George S. Patton

THREE

■ ■ TWELVE PEOPLE IN THE NEW YORK area died from
■ ■ heat-related causes, a workman on the site collapsed
from dehydration, the weather finally broke, and I kept returning to Dr. Gabor. What choice did I have? I could not go
through life without a voice.

"Let's go back to the war," he said on my next visit.

"I do not remember much."

"You said you were in Amsterdam for most of it."

I nodded.

"Your father was with the occupation?"

"I told you, my father was Dutch. We moved back before the war. June 1937."

"Why?"

"Business opportunities."

"And when the war came?"

He would not let go of it. What did a Dutchman who had lived in Germany do in Amsterdam during the war?

"I was in Auschwitz." My voice rasped like a key turning in a rusted lock.

He looked up from the yellow legal pad. "As a guard or a prisoner?"

The fucking son-of-a-bitch.

"A prisoner."

The son-of-a-bitch blinked. The features rearranged themselves into the look. I had not seen it in some time. The war had been over for seven years. I was not the only one eager to forget it. But there was a time when I knew that look like the back of my hand, or the number on my arm. It was full of pity, and shame, and one thing more. Dislike. He did not hate me as he had when he imagined me turning in Jews and beating up Dutch, but he did not like me for having been there either.

Just remember, where you've been, what you've seen, it's not going to endear you to people.

"I thought you said you were in Amsterdam."

"I was. Until August of '44. August fourth, to be precise. I was arrested and sent to Westerbork, then to Auschwitz."

"For what reason?"

"You think they needed a reason?"

"If you were Jewish, no, but if you weren't, there was usually some pretext. Political activity. Homosexuality."

"Not that."

He put down his pen and leaned back in his chair. "Political activity?"

They had rounded up thirty or forty resistance fighters, but somehow word got out that there was a Jew among them. The SS came crashing through the cars of the train, swinging their rifles, using their fists, howling take down your pants, take down your pants. Only in German, which I refuse to speak, even in my head.

"Political activity," I agreed.

"Tell me about it."

I shrugged. "I really cannot remember. Whether you believe me or not."

"I believe you. It's a common phenomenon among people who have been in the camps."

"I am not like them," I rasped.

"You mean you're not Jewish?"

"I mean I refuse to live in the past. I do not talk about it. I never even think about it. When my mind travels back, it stops at the gangplank to the ship I came over on."

"All right, tell me about that."

You could not understand, Doctor. You, who arrived before the war with your medical degree and your steamer trunks and your books. Or did you have to leave the trunks and the books behind? Were you only a step ahead of Hitler? But still in the nick of time, you clever Hungarian devil. For those of us who came after, it was a different story.

The sun beat down from a white sky and sparked off the oily river. Gulls shrieked like mad old women, the ship's whistle split the salt-smelling air, and people shouted at each other in a babel of languages. Even if you could not understand the words, you interpreted the excitement, and the terror. I was sure someone was going to be pushed overboard or trampled underfoot in the rush to get down the gangplank and onto American soil.

It was even worse in the customs shed. The sound of scraping wheels and thudding suitcases and human voices rattled the tin walls. Men moved through the heat like underwater swimmers. Women fanned themselves with hats and handkerchiefs and documents. Children cried. An old man fainted. And at the far end of the shed a shaft of sunlight poured through an opening in the metal wall. It was blinding. It was America.

The crowd churned. People searched for the proper queue. Officials pointed here and directed there and called for interpreters. Volunteers from a dozen different agencies tried to help, lost their patience, and shouted at the terrified people they had come to aid. I found my place at the end of a line. It moved a few inches, then stopped as men and women hunted for documents in satchels and pockets and linings of coats too heavy for the heat-dizzy morning. Suddenly a woman began to keen. She wanted her child. Where was her child? Women shouted. Men rushed to the openings for the gangplanks and looked frantically down at the engine-swirled water. A shout went up from the other side of the pier. Here he is! Here he is! The woman raced to her child, scooped him up, put him down, shook him, embraced him, shook him again. People turned away. They had troubles of their own.

The line continued to crawl forward. The longer I waited, the more jittery I became. Something could always go wrong. Rules changed. Papers that were adequate when the boat left Bremen might be insufficient by the time it docked in New York. I kept taking out my documents and checking them. I had not been able to keep from doing that on the ship, and the papers were smudged with fingerprints and wrinkled from being carried close to my body. The Certificate of Identity in Lieu of a Passport was in the worst shape. You see, Doctor, some of us did not have the real thing. At the time, I still considered it a lack. It never occurred to me it would be an advantage.

This is to certify that **Peter van Pels** . . .

I had held my breath as the secretary in the camp typed the information into the blanks.

. . . born at **Osnabruck, Germany** on **8th** of **November, 1926, male, unmarried,** intends to immigrate to the United States of America.

Height **6** ft. **2** in.

Hair **Brown** Eyes **Blue**

Distinguishing marks or features: **scar on right arm above wrist.**

They had listed the scar from the rat bite on my right arm, but not the number on my left. There had been too many of those to be distinguishing.

Applicant declares he has never been convicted of breaking any laws.

The hinges of the barn door creak. Animals stir and snort and paw. The old man snores.

But I had never been convicted of anything.

I put the papers back in the breast pocket of my jacket, safe from harm, ready to be produced on demand.

There were still half a dozen people in front of me. Perhaps I had contracted a disease aboard ship, and some telltale sign would give me away. Perhaps someone had lodged a complaint against me. People were always making up stories. This one had been a capo. That one was a communist. So-and-so had run a thriving black market operation. They did it to advance themselves, and settle scores, and because they had to find somewhere to rest the backbreaking rage they carried around with them.

I was getting close now. There was only one person in front of me. The customs officer took the man's passport and visa and stood staring down at the documents. "Wishwzzz . . ." His voice trailed off in a buzz of consonants. He shook his head. "That's not a name, it's a curse." He wrote something on the documents, stamped them, and handed them back. "Welcome to the United States, sir." He hissed the last word, but the man simply took the papers, nodded several times to show his gratitude, and moved away. I stepped up to the table and handed over my papers smartly, but not too smartly. No hint of clicking heels or snappy salutes. I did not want to give him the wrong idea.

He took the Certificate of Identity from my hand that, to my amazement, was not shaking and looked down at it. "Van Pels. Now, there's a good American name. As American as Stuyvesant. New York used to be Nieuw Amsterdam, you know. Brooklyn was originally Breuckelen. Harlem, Haarlem." He murmured something else. He was still looking down at the certificate, and he had spoken under his breath, but I knew the words. I knew them in English and French and Dutch and German. I could probably recognize them in half a dozen other languages I did not speak.

"Not one of the chosen people," he had muttered.

I wondered if it was a joke, or a test. I watched as he went on studying the Certificate. When I had first seen it, I had been surprised. I still could not get over it. German and Dutch papers, even DP documents, listed the religion of the bearer. The Certificate of Identity in Lieu of a Passport issued by the United States Consulate General recorded only how tall I was, and whether I had any distinguishing marks on my body, and if I had been convicted of a crime. What a country!

The officer looked up from the document. I waited for him to realize his mistake. On the boat they had all taken me for one of them.

"You spend enough time in this place, Mr. van Pels, you begin to think we're nothing but a dumping ground for the world's garbage. Makes you wonder what our boys fought for." He stamped the Certificate of Identity. "I must have processed a hundred immigrants this morning, and you're the first one I might let marry my sister." He winked and held the document out to me. Take it, Mr. van Pels. Take your good Dutch-American name, and your Certificate of Identity that lists no religion, and go out into America as one of the people not chosen.

I had been thinking about it for years. I had made up my mind a dozen, perhaps a hundred times. I had calculated the odds, and considered the dangers, and figured the practicalities. But I had never expected the option to be handed to me so easily. There was no proof of what I was. There was not a trace of who I had been. The Red Cross did not even list me as a survivor. According to their records, I had probably died on the forced march, or just after it in Mauthausen. They might have been right, if the German soldier, who looked no less Aryan than the SS officers driving us west, no more humane than that bastard of a farmer in the barn, had not, on some whim I will never understand and he probably did not comprehend at the time, given me that moldy piece of bread. Or maybe he did understand. The end of the war was in sight. Maybe he was making his own bargain with the future. But it was all speculation, about the man's motives, about the fate of a boy named Peter van Pels.

I lifted my arm to take the Certificate. My sleeve pulled back only an inch, not enough to reveal the number to the officer, but I knew it was there. They had not listed it on the Certificate, because it was not a distinguishing feature, but it could still give me away. I wondered what the smirking officer who muttered anti-Semitic slurs under his breath would say if I took off my jacket, and rolled up my sleeve, and showed him that I was just another piece of the world's garbage. But not everyone in the camps had been Jewish. The number told where I had been, but not who I was. Someday I could even have it removed. I had heard there were doctors who did that.

I stood staring at the thumbed documents in the customs officer's hand. I did not believe in God. How could I, after where I had been and what I had seen? I did not even recall the trappings.

The sweat beaded my upper lip, and poured out of my armpits, and ran down my sides. My shirt was drenched. My underwear was a wet rag sticking to my belly and buttocks and the real problem. The proof of who I was. The cut of Abraham, the sign of the covenant, the incision of my infancy, the missing foreskin, the incontrovertible proof of me.

I stood staring at the man in the uniform who had mistaken me for a gentile, remembering other men in uniform who had been just as inefficient. No, not remembering, because the story did not belong to me, though somehow in the retelling and reimagining it had become mine.

The man who told the story had been rounded up and put on a train in a sweep of Polish resistance fighters—some communists, some Catholics, all anti-Semites, the teller had sworn—but word had gone through the cars that there was a Jew among them. And right behind the word came the officers, shouting obscenities, slamming rifle butts, howling at the men to drop their pants. The man who had told the story had sprung to the front of the line and begun tugging at his buttons. A rifle butt had crashed into his chest. He had fallen to the floor and rolled back into the huddle of bruised, beaten, uncircumcised resistance fighters, undiscovered.

But I was in America now. Here men in uniform did not order other men to take down their pants. Here men in uniform smiled, even while they muttered insults under their breath, and said welcome and good luck and you are going to feel right at home.

But sooner or later I would take down my pants. I could still see the *Life* magazine picture of the sailor bending the nurse over backward. Sooner or later, I would give myself away. Jew-hating knew no sex. There was a man in the camp who had been turned in by his Aryan mistress. Probably more than one, but he was the one I knew.

That was what I was thinking the first time I saw Susannah. Or maybe I was thinking that because I had already seen her out of the corner of my eye.

How long in this Bible-reading till we get to the story of the bathing Susanna?

And what do they mean by Sodom and Gomorrah?

Anne, Peter, will you two be serious!

The first thing I noticed was her hair. It had taken me longer to get used to seeing women with hair than it had to seeing women without it. What do you make of that, Doctor? Susannah's hair was dark blond and silky. She wore it long then, so it spilled over one velvet-lashed eye, like the pictures of Veronica Lake from before the war. I had read, in *Life* again, that at the beginning of the war, the movie star, in a patriotic gesture, had shorn that silky curtain every man wanted to get his hands in. Not since Samson had a haircut had such dire consequences. Overnight Veronica was a has-been. But Susannah had hair like Veronica's before she cut it, and a small sweet nose that stopped just short of snub, and those straight white teeth that would have made Dr. Pfeffer weep with wonder. The teeth, as I said, ran in the family. She was smiling down at a boy, whom I recognized from the group of orphans on the boat, and in that smile I saw a large and loving clan that had been smiling back at her since infancy. There was an identification pin on her small pointy left breast, though I was not close enough to read her name or that of the agency where she volunteered. Later we would argue about that. No, not argue, disagree.

She must have felt me watching her, because she looked up. My eye caught hers. I saw the color seep into her cheeks.

Is Mouschi a boy or a girl?

He's a tom, Anne.

That was when it came to me. A mistress might know. A whore would know. But a nice girl would not have an inkling. I could take down my pants and still keep my secret.

I took the Certificate of Identity in lieu of the real thing
from the customs officer, put it in the pocket of my sweat-limp
trousers, and started toward the square of blinding sunlight at
the end of the shed. As I stepped outside into my new life, I
felt curiously weightless. I felt light enough to float away. That
was what I did when Werner Pfeffer asked me for news of his
late father.

"I know nothing of a Fritz Pfeffer or a family called Frank,"
I said and disappeared across Twelfth Avenue into America.

"On October 23—one day after the 'Aryanization' decree—a notary . . . was asked, at Otto's instigation, to register a new company. . . . Kugler was given as its managing director and J. A. Gies . . . a supervisory director. . . . The paid-up shares . . . were issued to Kugler and Gies. The business was thus wholly 'Aryan,' at least officially, but in practice the actual ownership of the company remained vested in Otto Frank."

—*The Diary of Anne Frank:*
The Critical Edition

FOUR

■ ■ WHEN THE DOOR TO HARRY'S OFFICE opened and he
■ ■ stepped into the hall, I knew the timing was not accidental. He had been waiting for me to come out of my own office. He wanted to talk to me, but he did not want to appear as if he wanted to talk to me. If I had intended to take advantage of Harry when we started out, which I definitely had not, it would not have been difficult.

He fell in step beside me, a balding man with a perpetual purple shadow on his jaw and a bulky bottom-heavy body that reminded me of my daughter's rubber Shmoo. The toy is weighted at the feet so that every time Abigail pushes it over, it pops back up.

"How's the throat, pal?" When I first knew Harry, he used to call me boychick, but after he found out I wasn't Jewish, he switched to pal. He also stopped peppering his conversation with Yiddish expressions, at least when he was with me. His voice now was elaborately casual, but I knew he was worried. Banks and businesses do not like to extend credit to invalids. No one wants to buy a house from a man who is here today and gone tomorrow.

"Getting better every day," I said, as we came out of the building into the parking lot.

"Great, great." He reached up and pounded my shoulder. "So they found the problem?"

They did not exactly find it, pal. They just named it. Aphonia, Dr. Gabor called it. I had no intention of telling Harry that. I had not even told him about Dr. Gabor. Harry is not a callous man. He has, if anything, a reverence for illness. He speaks of heart attacks and strokes in hushed tones. He does not use the word cancer at all. The big C is as close as he gets to naming it. Harry believes in the power of words. He might even appreciate aphonia, so musical and medical in the same breath. But then I would have to explain that it is not a physical illness, only the description of the absence of one. That would distress him. He prefers his diseases to be observable under a microscope, or detectable on an X-ray, or measurable by a machine.

"No need to worry," I told him. "It is not communicative. I mean communicable," I corrected myself and laughed to show it was a joke.

He smoothed the dark hair he had begun, in the past year, to comb across the crown of his head. "The only reason I ask, pal, is that people keep asking me. I ran into George Johnson this morning. He wanted to know how my partner was, and I didn't know what the hell to tell him."

"Tell George and everyone else I am just fine. Getting better every day. You can hear how much stronger my voice is," I croaked into the dusk.

We had reached Harry's car, a robin's egg blue Coupe de Ville, hot off the assembly line, and the sight of that blinding chrome and those curvy fenders that would not be out of place in a burlesque house took his mind off my problems.

"Is she a beauty or is she a beauty?" he asked. I agreed that she was. He pulled open the door and folded himself into the soft upholstery that smelled good enough to eat. "Maybe you should take up these," he said, as he drew a crushed package of Lucky Strikes from his pocket and pushed the lighter into the winking dashboard. "It wouldn't help your throat, but at least it would give you an excuse for it."

He held the glowing tip of the lighter to the cigarette, inhaled deeply, and exhaled. The aroma of tobacco floated toward me, sweeter than the smell of new leather, stronger than the acrid fumes of the passing traffic. I grabbed on to the baby blue door of Harry's car to keep from doubling over.

You know why we have no money for food, Putti? Because it goes up in smoke. The smoke from your filthy cigarettes.

The pain disappeared as suddenly as it had come, but I knew I had not imagined it. I stood in the gathering twilight sweating with fear. Dr. Gabor and the other doctors were wrong. The pain had been too sharp to be psychosomatic. It must be the symptom of a fatal disease.

■   ■   ■   ■

I WAS ten minutes late for my appointment with Dr. Gabor. I blamed it on Harry.

"My partner had some matters he wanted to go over," I said.

"Problems?"

"Just business."

"You and your partner get along?"

I nodded.

"How did you come to go into business together?"

In the DP camp, if they talked about the past at all, they talked about ifs. If I had been in the front of the line that morning and not at the end. If I had hung back instead of stepping forward. If I had not been the first to start unbuttoning my pants when the SS came through the train. Gradually the ifs led to theories. I survived because I was careful. I lived because I took chances. But beneath those convictions about the effectiveness of certain behavior, going hand-in-contradictory-hand with them, was a fearsome respect for chance. Chance brought me together with Harry Wolfe—"Like the animal, but with an *e*," he said when he introduced himself— but I took advantage of him. I mean of it, of the situation.

"Harry owned a parcel of land," I rasped. "I had saved a little money and was looking for a business."

It was not a lie. I had saved money, every penny I had made waiting tables and driving a cab. But that was not why Harry took me on. He did not need my money. He needed me. That was not my fault.

"He was the first friend I made in America."

Harry had been a regular at the restaurant where I worked.

That was before he married. He used to come in three or four times a week, occasionally with a girl or another man, but usually alone. He kept company with his papers and documents and brochures. I used to sneak glances at them as I served his dinner and cleared his plates. "Guidelines of the Federal Housing Administration." "Prefabrication Methods and the Rate of Housing Starts." "Mortgage Financing as the Key to High Production."

One night he caught me looking at them. "Wave of the future." He tapped the brochure with his knife. "This housing shortage isn't going away anytime soon."

I nodded and went off to take care of other tables.

"Since the war," he said when I returned, "every Joe and his little woman want a house of their own. More to the point, the government says they're entitled to a house of their own. It's part of the GI Bill of Rights."

I knew about the Bill of Rights. I had already begun to study for my citizenship exam, though I would not be eligible for more than four years. But strange as it seems to me now, I had never heard of the GI Bill of Rights.

"You know where they want their houses?" Harry said when I returned with his coffee and pie. I was not hovering. I was merely doing my job. "Not here in the city where the kids will grow up not even knowing what a blade of grass looks like, unless their parents schlep them to Prospect Park. Not in the towns they came from where the houses are old and need work and have one lousy bathroom with worse plumbing for the whole family. They want them in the suburbs. Brand-new, never-before-lived-in houses in spanking-new suburbs. Where the kids have a whole yard to play in. And the little woman has a shiny new kitchen with all the latest appliances. And you don't have to worry about your property values, because all the houses look just like yours, and all your neighbors are just like you, or at least free, white, and twenty-one."

I told him I had read that a couple of men named Levitt were planning something like that on Long Island. His eyes, which were set a little too close to instill trust, narrowed, as if he were taking me in for the first time, and I knew he was surprised. I was not just a greenie waiting tables. I might even be smarter than I looked.

Remember when he first arrived, Anne, that morning when we were all at breakfast? What a dope, you said. He won't amount to much.

Margot! I never said that.

A week later Harry told me he had an extra ticket to the Yankees and the Dodgers at Yankee Stadium and wanted to know if I was interested. I did not like taking off a whole night from work, but something about Harry smacked of opportunity. My boss was always saying that if I kept on the way I was going, I could count on a job waiting tables for the rest of my life. I told Harry I had never been to an American baseball game and would like very much to go.

"Good," he said, "only it's not baseball, it's pro football. Don't worry, boychick, it's a normal mistake. Anyone could make it."

After that, Harry got in the habit of lingering until the other customers had left. Then he would tell me to pour myself a cup of coffee and cut myself a slice of pie on him, and take a load off my feet. You did not have to be a greenie living alone in a basement room with an eye out for the main chance to know Harry Wolfe was a lonely man. I would do as he said, and we would talk. Or rather Harry would talk and I would listen.

Harry was to me what night school was to the waiters and cab-drivers who were in less of a rush. He was where I learned that the GI Bill of Rights made it possible for returning servicemen to go to college, and start businesses, and, here was the best part, buy houses, or, as Harry put it, become homeowners. I learned about government incentives for bankers to issue low-interest mortgages to veterans, and government guarantees that the bankers would recover a portion of their investment if the veterans defaulted. I learned about the vagaries of building codes that could dictate to Harry the pitch of a roof or the thickness of a wall, and the selfishness of county planning boards who were more interested in luring tax-paying corpora-tions than honest-to-goodness vets, who would need schools and sewers and other expensive services. I learned more about the Levitts, who were Harry's professional heroes and would become his personal nemesis. The Levitts, Harry said, were Jews. I registered the information, but I did not react to it. And most important of all, I learned how, thanks to all those gov-ernment programs, bankers would make production advances to builders as work progressed, so someone like Harry—even someone like me, Harry added with a wink—did not need a bundle to go into business on his own.

But gradually the word *when* began to creep into Harry's sure thing, and then *if* began to replace *when*. Not the instructive *if* of past experience that the DPs had clung to like rabbits' feet, but the regretful *if* of lost opportunity. The bankers were stalling him, he said. The local planning boards would not give him the time of day. Every time he changed the architectural plans or specifications to meet one code, some son-of-a-bitch came up with another he had never heard of.

"Makes you wonder what we fought a war for," Harry said one night as we were walking up Fulton Street. The wind knifed off the East River and sliced through us. Steel grates rattled on the windows of closed shops. An emaciated Christmas tree grew out of a metal trash can.

"What do you mean?"

"I mean we sent millions of guys over there to knock out Hitler, but nobody lifts a finger to fight it at home."

"It?"

"Anti-Semitism, boychick. Jew-hating, Jew-baiting, Jews need not apply, no dogs and Jews, get those sheeny bastard Christ-killers out of here."

"What about the Levitts? They get the loans. They get planning board approval." I tried to sound nonchalant, like a man who abhorred injustice, rather than a victim with a vested interest.

"That's just the problem. The Levitts have bought up half the potato farms on Long Island. I want to build twenty, thirty homes. They're talking two or three thousand. Maybe more."

Harry underestimated his heroes that night. Their first development eventually numbered more than seventeen thousand units. I should have told Dr. Gabor that. He would not have been so in awe of my accomplishments. But I had no intention of telling him about my arrangement with Harry. Not even my wife knew the original reason we went into business together.

"The point is," Harry went on, "the Levitts just make it harder for little guys like me. People look at them and say, 'Uh-oh, the Jews are taking over the building industry.' 'Watch out, the Yids are buying up the area.' Then they start stonewalling guys like me."

We walked on for another block or two. I asked if he was sure he was not imagining it. He said he knew it when it hit him on the head. I asked about the ten acres he had an option on in New Jersey. He described the location again. I asked a few more details, though I already knew them by heart. But all the time I was questioning him, I was arguing with myself. I could not do it. It was not right. But other people had.

The gentlemen from Frankfurt are coming.

Kugler will have to see them.

Kugler's not up to it.

Kugler's all we have. It's an Aryan business now, remember.

No, I could not do it. It would be wrong.

We stopped at a corner to wait for the light to change. Another Christmas tree sprouted from another trash can. Silver tinsel clung to the branches for dear life.

On the other hand, I would not be hurting anyone. I would be doing Harry a service. I would also be striking a blow for justice. And for Jews. Or a Jew. At least, I would outwit the odds stacked against him. The more I thought about it, the more right it seemed. The more I turned the plan around in my mind, the more foolproof I knew it was. We walked on, Harry hunched under the weight of his worries, me galloping beside him on a white horse, my armor clanking and rattling in the winter wind.

"Maybe I can help," I said.

He stopped walking as I started to explain the plan. I was surprised I remembered the details my father and Mr. Frank had worked out with the employees. I had forgotten so much else. Harry would incorporate, and I would buy some of the shares with the money I had already saved, and V, for van Pels,

and W, for Wolfe, Construction would have one gentile partner, me, who would be extremely visible, and one Jewish,
Harry, who could fade into the background when necessary.

"Well, I'll be a son-of-a-bitch," he kept repeating as we stood
in the pasty light of a neon sign for Hebrew National frank-
furters. "Well, I'll be a son-of-a-bitch."

"You could have fooled me," he said half an hour later,
when we were sitting at a greasy table in an all-night restaurant.
In the glare of the overhead lights, his stubbled jaw look sore,
and his eyes were wary. Who could blame him? A man does
not sign away half his dream without second thoughts. But I
had gone over the plan several times, and he had not been able
to find a flaw.

"Fooled you about what?" I asked. "That a greenie straight
off the boat could come up with a plan like this?" I could use
the word now that it was receding into my past.

"Nah, I always knew you were a smart kid. Maybe that was
why I figured you were Jewish. I thought you changed your
name, but I guess I should have known. It's one thing to go
from Moscowitz to Miller, but van Pels is too swanky. You start
out life Rabinowitz, you don't suddenly become Roosevelt.
Not that it makes a difference. To me, I mean."

It made no difference to him, but suddenly there were no
more Jewish jokes. "So these three rabbis meet in a whore-
house . . ." There were no more slurs. "If that guy thinks he
can Jew me down . . ." There were no more boasts. "You
should have seen me Jew that guy down." He still liked me. He
must have trusted me. But he was less easy with me.

The men he had been complaining about were a different
story. The bankers were happy to make government-backed

loans to Peter van Pels, and the local councilmen and aldermen picked up my calls and pocketed my payoffs. Some of them wondered how I had got caught up in that mess in Europe, but nobody wanted to ask. They were relieved to find a good Christian who had stood up to Hitler and to be able to deal with him rather than some of the others. I was living proof they had nothing against foreigners. I was, George Johnson joked after we signed the papers for the first loan, their own private Marshall Plan.

"I had money to invest," I told Dr. Gabor, "but it was more than that."

"What do you mean?"

"I have always been good with my hands."

"Surely you've progressed beyond that."

"It was my idea that put us ahead of the competition." If Harry ever forgot that, I was there to remind him. I was more than just a front man.

"What idea was that?"

"We build a bigger house and sell it for the same price. And not by cutting quality."

"Then how do you do it?" The owl eyes regarded me with interest. He had the intellectual's secret respect for practical expertise.

"It was simple," I told him. It was, as I said, so simple I had been amazed no one else had thought of it. But then no one else had Susannah. At least not in those days.

"Space inside a house is cheap. About one-third as expensive as the overall cost per square foot. And it does not require more plumbing or wiring or windows. The others are catching on now, but we were the first to do it."

"And you say the idea just came to you?"

"Out of the blue," I answered.

More accurately, the slate blue of Susannah's eyes, but Susannah was one more subject I had no intention of taking up with the doctor.

"Business is good," I went on. "The company is solid. Whatever is wrong with my voice does not have to do with that."

He sat watching me. The moment of curiosity had passed. The balance between us had shifted again.

"Have you ever sought psychiatric help in the past, Mr. van Pels?"

I shook my head no.

"Not even when you developed the tremors."

"I knew the doctor was wrong. The last thing I wanted was to go back to that DP camp."

"What about the camp? A psychological evaluation was usually part of the process of getting a visa."

He was a clever devil, all right. They called it an evaluation. Obstacle course would be more like it. The psychological exam was even more treacherous than the physical. At least there you knew what they were looking for. A lesion on the lung. A spirochete in the blood. But who knew what these civilians with their incomprehensible titles—psychiatric social worker, master of social work, doctor of psychology—were after? Who could guess what answer would keep you out, what word would give you away? Who could even concentrate on the questions in that office where SS officers had once issued their orders and kept their records? That was where they held the evaluations. I often wondered who had got the bright idea of housing a DP camp in an old SS barracks. Was it a cutup with a wicked sense of irony or merely a pragmatist who had spotted a prime physical plant? Probably the latter. The United Nations Relief and Rehabilitation Agency ran the operation, but America called the shots.

As I stepped into the office, I heard the gunshot crack of boots snapping to attention. As I took the seat I was directed to, I heard the guttural growl of threats and the sibilant whisper of lethal secret plans. But the man sitting across the desk from me that morning was not a German officer. He was an American civilian. STANLEY MINTZ, M.S.W. the brass nameplate on his desk said. He stroked the nameplate with his fingers as he asked me questions.

"Do you feel guilty?"

"Guilty?" I repeated.

"Guilty." Mintz lifted his fingers from the nameplate, picked up an English-German dictionary, and began leafing through it.

"I know what the word means." The anger in my voice frightened me. It was a luxury I could not afford.

Mintz put down the dictionary and leaned back in his chair. "You're not going to get anywhere with a chip on your shoulder, young man."

I did not answer.

"Well, do you? Feel guilty, I mean. There's nothing to be ashamed of. It's a perfectly normal response."

I sat staring at the nameplate. It was a long metal triangle with a wide base and a sharp top. I felt the weight in my hand. I saw it crashing into Mintz's head. The blood burst into bloom like a flower. Mintz's eyes opened, wide and dead as coins, just like the eyes of the man in the barn.

Forget guilt, let's talk about revenge, I should have said.

"No," I told Stanley Mintz.

"No," I repeated to Dr. Gabor now. "I never sought psychiatric help. Why would I?"

"That he [Peter] is handsome I needn't say, for
everyone who sees him knows that. His hair is wonderful—a wealth of fine brown curls. He has gray-
blue eyes."

—*Tales from the House Behind:
Fables, Personal Reminiscences,
and Short Stories*, by Anne Frank

"I now have a better understanding of why he
[Peter] always hugs Mouschi so tightly. He obviously needs affection too."

—*The Diary of a Young Girl*,
by Anne Frank, February 16, 1944

"In the meantime, a shadow has fallen on my happiness. For a long time I've had the feeling that
Margot likes Peter."

—*The Diary of a Young Girl*,
by Anne Frank, March 20, 1944

F I V E

SUSANNAH WAS SITTING IN THE family room when I
got home from my appointment with Dr. Gabor that
evening. I was not surprised to see her. My wife and her sister
are always in and out of each other's houses.

"Madeleine is upstairs with the girls," she said. "I'm just killing
time. Norman's car is in the shop, and I have to pick him up."

Without getting up from the sofa where she was sitting with a magazine in her lap, she lifted a cheek to be kissed. I obliged. The gesture was innocent, bereft of memory, like so much of my life.

"How's your voice?" she asked. "It sounds as if it's getting better."

I had said only hello, and that in a hoarse whisper, but she is a good woman, my sister-in-law. That was what came between us.

"Madeleine told me about the doctor," she went on.

I had wondered if Madeleine had mentioned Gabor to her family. My guess was that she had kept it from her mother, who found me sufficiently peculiar without a professional diagnosis, but bragged to her sister, the psychology major, who could only envy a husband so fearless he would delve into the depths of his own being.

"I think it's so brave of you. Most men would rather die than go to a psychiatrist." She ran a hand through her silky hair, and I wondered, though I almost never do, what it would have been like if I had married her instead of her sister.

We met at a party a few months after Harry and I went into business together. I never would have had the courage to approach her, I never would have had the nerve to go to the party, if I had still been waiting tables and driving a cab. Walking up Broadway that night through the coronas of mist that hung from the streetlights, listening to the sizzle of tires on wet pavement, I still had second thoughts. I would not know anyone except the man from the night school class in real estate that I was finally taking, and I barely knew him. The place would be full of college men, and war veterans, and strangers who would either want to know who I was and where

I had come from, or would not. I would feel either trapped or ostracized. But the man from the night school class had said there would be girls. Lots of them.

I shouldered my way into the room. It was like diving into a dream of plenty. All around me hair shimmered, and lashes fluttered, and tongues darted over lipsticked mouths. It was so crowded I could not move without colliding with a sweet-slung hip or glancing off a jiggling breast. I felt as if I would drown in it. Then I saw her.

Actually, I recognized her. She was the girl from the customs shed, though I did not tell her that. I wanted to pass as a man of the world, not an immigrant off the boat.

"Do you want to know what I thought the first time I saw you?" she would ask later, when we were tangled together on the gold brocade sofa of her parents' living room. We were so sure we had a future, we were beginning to build a past.

"What?" I would gasp above the importuning of that traitor in my trousers.

"That you were different."

I did not tell her I had no desire to be different. When she said it that way, I did. But I still did not say anything about seeing her in the customs shed. Different was all right. Greenie was another story. Greenie was the kiss of death, or so I thought at the time.

All around us people were falling in love. People are always falling in love, but that year they were doing it differently. During the war they had fallen in love because there was no tomorrow. Now they were falling in love because there was tomorrow and next year and the year after that.

We sat in darkened movie theaters, her smooth shoulders

fitting into the curve of my arm, my gray flannel knee—I said clothes are the easiest camouflage—pressed against her nylon-stockinged thigh. We walked the streets, our fingers linked together in a pickproof lock against the world. We closed our-selves into the tiny soundproof booths of record stores and listened to the new long-playing records, while she swooned to Beethoven and snapped her fingers to Stan Getz playing with the Woody Herman Band, and I explained the magic behind thirty-three revolutions per minute. We did things she had never done before, and felt things we were sure no one in the world had ever felt before, and murmured each other's names and *oh* and *yes* and *please* and finally, because she was a nice girl and planned to stay that way until she was married, *no*.

Father says in these matters, the man always takes the active role, and the woman has to set the limits.

I was glad now that she had said no. I know there are men who find the idea of sleeping with their wives' sisters titillating, but I am not one of them. To me it would be merely chaotic.

One Sunday we drove to New Jersey in the '39 Chevy Harry sold me after he slipped a couple of hundred dollars to the dealer under the table to get one of the new ones coming off the assembly line. I wanted to show Susannah the houses I was building.

When we pulled up to the muddy site spiked with raw wooden frames rising from rutted earth, she let out a small cry. I asked what was wrong. She said the scene reminded her of the photographs of bombed-out cities that still filled the pages of *Life* each week. I should have known then what I was up against. None of this let's-sweep-the-war-under-the-rug-and-get-on-with-life fecklessness for my girl. I reminded her those skeletons were remnants of destruction, these were under construction.

Once we made our way across planks laid over the mud and were standing beneath an unfinished roof open to a metallic sky, alone in the half privacy of the two-by-fours, even she turned away from the cloud-shrouded spring afternoon toward a rosy future.

"The sofa goes there," she said, moving around the soon-to-be living room, "and two chairs, one for you, one for me, over here." She stopped. "There's no room for an end table. You'll need an end table with a good lamp to read the evening paper. And your books." Like her sister after her, she could not get over the fact that I had read not only Dickens and Thackeray, but also Goethe and Schiller, in the original, as she put it. "I'm sorry to tell you this, Peter, but you're going to have to make the living room bigger."

I did not tell her the skeletal room was the same size as the equivalent rooms in similar houses in comparable developments. If it was too small for Susannah, it would have to be larger. Suddenly I knew how to make it that way without increasing costs. And now we were standing in one of the results.

My sister-in-law looked at her watch, stood, and smoothed her skirt with the silky self-loving gesture of a cat grooming, and I knew that just as a moment ago I had wondered what it would have been like if I had married her instead of her sister, she was remembering that she had broken my heart. At the time, I had almost believed the phrase, though by then I should have known none of my organs was that fragile.

It was the summer after she had graduated from Barnard. She was living in her parents' solid Tudor house on a leafy street not

far from where we were now and working at a day camp for
refugee children. I had said, when she had taken the job, that she
had a calling, or at least a soft spot, for those children.

"What do you mean?" she asked, and that was when I finally
told her about the first time I saw her, months before the party.
I was far enough away from the customs shed by then to be
able to own up to it, or at least part of it.

"But I was never there," she said.

"You must have forgotten."

"I did some volunteer work for the Hebrew Immigrant Aid
Society," she insisted, "but I never went down to the piers to
meet the ships."

I let it go. The last thing I wanted was to argue with
Susannah, though we argued that summer night.

We had been to the movies, and because it was a pleasant
evening and her parents lived not in a suburban development
without sidewalks, but in a town where people could still walk
to the dry cleaner's and the drugstore and the movie theater,
we walked that night. We were on our way home when she
mentioned it. Overhead, canopies of oak and elm and maple
blotted out the stars, and on both sides of us darkened houses
dreamed silently in the summer heat. Our twinned shadows
spilled out from our feet, growing long and emaciated as we
left the arc of one streetlight, shrinking back into proportion
as we entered the sphere of another.

"I heard the funniest thing today." Her voice was so soft it
barely troubled the night.

"What was that?"

"A girl at the day camp knows your partner Harry. I think
she likes him."

"Wonderful," I said. I wanted Harry to be happy. I owed him a great deal.

"I don't know if she likes him that much, but that wasn't what was funny."

"What was?"

"Harry told her you weren't Jewish."

She had not raised her voice, but I could feel the air tremble. We walked a few more steps. Our shadows began to fade before us and spill out behind.

"I told her she must have misunderstood him." Her voice had grown no louder, but there was an importuning undercurrent. "Or else he was talking about someone else."

We were standing directly under the light now, casting no shadow at all. She lifted her face to me. Just above the bridge of the small snub nose, which I did not at the time know had been surgically altered, a single furrow worried her creamy forehead.

"He was talking about someone else, wasn't he?"

"Does it matter?"

She dropped my hand. "Don't be silly, Peter. Of course it matters."

I took her hand and tried to start walking again, but she stood her ground.

"Are you saying you're not Jewish?"

"I am not saying anything. You are, and Harry, and the girl at the day camp."

She tugged her hand out of mine. "This isn't a joke."

"Of course it is."

She took my hand and started walking again. "Thank heavens. For a minute you had me worried."

We walked on in silence, trying to catch up with our shadows.

"Still, I don't think you should joke about something like that. Or Harry shouldn't."

We kept walking. I still said nothing. She stopped again. "Is it a joke or isn't it?"

I turned to her. We were equidistant between street lamps again, and her face was in shadows. I hoped mine was too. "I find it funny that you find it so important."

"Of course it's important."

"I am the same person, one way or another."

"That's not the point."

"What is the point?"

"Why didn't you tell me?"

"Tell you what?"

"That you're not . . ." she stopped. "Peter, are you teasing me? If you are, I'll never forgive you."

"I bet you will," I said and reached for her, but she took a step back.

"Just tell me. Are you or aren't you?" Now her voice disturbed the peace on that leafy silent street.

I tried to start walking again, but she was rooted to the spot. "Tell me the truth, Peter."

All I could tell her was my truth. I loved her, but I loved my own skin more. The next time they came, I would not be there.

"I am not."

Her intake of breath sounded like wind through the leaves overhead.

"It does not make any difference." I reached for her again. She stepped back again. "I would never interfere with your beliefs. I will even raise the children as Jews," I promised, though I knew I would not. The next time they came, my children would not be there either. I could not help the fact that their mother would be Jewish. I had never intended to fall in love with a Jew. Certainly I had not fallen in love with her because she was Jewish, no matter what Dr. Gabor said. But after we were married, after the children were born, I would find a way to erase the traces. I did not tell her that at the time.

She started to walk, her head turned away from me, her shoulders squared, her high heels eating up the pavement in furious little steps. The heels stretched her calves, and as she moved away from me, the sight of those muscles, pulled tight as an archer's bow, pierced my heart.

"I can't see you again," she said. "I'm sorry, but I just can't."

I lengthened my stride to keep up with her. "This is ridiculous."

"You don't understand."

"No, and I did not understand the Nazi racial laws that prohibited Jews and gentiles from consorting either."

"That's a horrible thing to say."

"Maybe, but true."

She stopped and turned to me. "It would break my parents' hearts."

"Your parents like me," I said, though I knew the statement was only half accurate. Her father liked me. Her mother, as I said, was not so easily taken in. It was one thing to bring over a couple of cousins after the war. It was something else to let your daughter, your firstborn, a beautiful girl, a smart girl, a girl who could have any man she wanted, marry one of them.

"I can't do it. I can't marry a gentile."

I stood trapped in the circle of sepulcher-white light. There was no way out. Even if I told her the truth, even if she believed me, it would only make things worse. Now I was merely a gentile, someone she could not marry. If I owned up, I would be a Jew who had passed, someone she could only despise.

She was crying now. "I can't help it, Peter. Maybe I could have before the war," she said, holding her tear-streaked face up to me like an offering. "It didn't seem so important then. But it does now." She took a handkerchief from her pocket and blew her sweet, surgically improved nose. "Hitler made a Jew of me."

What a coincidence, I wanted to howl into the night and wake all those smugly slumbering neighbors. He did the same to me.

January 7, 1941: Jews may not attend the cinema.

April 15, 1941: Jews must hand in their wireless sets.

May 31, 1941: Jews may not use swimming pools and public parks.

September 15, 1941: Jews may not visit zoos, cafés, restaurants, hotels, guesthouses, theaters, cabarets, concerts, libraries, and reading rooms.

January 23, 1942: Jews may not use motorcars.

May 29, 1942: Jews are prohibited from fishing.

July 6, 1942: Jews may not use telephones.

He had made Jews of us all, the devout and the doubting, the religious and the secular, the two-parent, four-grandparent, one-hundred-per-centers and those who had only a thin trickle of blood from some half-forgotten ancestor. But here in America it was a different story. Here you could play at being the butt of history. Here a girl whose shining hair had never been shaved, and whose tender flesh had never been tattooed, and whose pale pampered body had never been flung into the

mud to serve as a stepping-stone so officers would not soil
their freshly polished boots, could claim that Hitler had made a
Jew of her too. Standing on that easy street, watching her walk
away from me, I finally believed in a chosen people. It was not
the Jews.

HER SISTER Madeleine called me the next day. I had not spoken to her on the phone before, or if I had, I had been asking
for Susannah and had not noticed her sister's voice. It was as
thick and rich as chocolate, not the American chocolate of
Hershey Bars and Kisses, but a darker richer substance my
senses almost remembered from a distant safe-seeming childhood. She said that if I was half as miserable as Susannah, I
could use some cheering up. She said she would take me out
and get me drunk. It was not the sort of thing a nice girl was
supposed to say, and I was surprised and a little offended, but I
forgave her. I was already beginning to transfer allegiance. I did
not even have to transfer it. That night Susannah had taken me
home for the first time, I had fallen in love with the whole family. Even before that. I had been in thrall to them since I had
seen her smile in the customs shed that morning, no matter
what she said, and imagined the family that had been smiling
back at her all these years.

Madeleine and I were married the following summer, right
after her graduation. She did not care that I was not Jewish.
Hitler, she said, had made an atheist of her.

As for the secret in my trousers, I had been right about a
nice girl's not knowing. We were married for three months
before she realized I was circumcised. By then I knew that in

America, unlike Europe, some gentiles were. I told her my parents had visited America on their honeymoon, and since I was conceived here, they decided to pay tribute to local custom. I never talked about my mother and father, and the story delighted her.

"Tell Madeleine I'll call her tomorrow," Susannah said now. She went up on her toes to plant a chaste goodbye kiss on my cheek, and suddenly I knew the answer to my idle question. If I had married her instead of her sister, with whom she was locked in a loving lifelong rivalry, it would have made little difference. That did not mean I did not love my wife.

"It would be terrible if my diary were lost."
—Anne Frank, quoted in *The Stolen Legacy
of Anne Frank: Meyer Levin, Lillian Hellman,
and the Staging of the Diary*, by Ralph Melnick

S I X

DR. GABOR RARELY ASKED ABOUT my voice, but he asked that evening. "Do you notice any improvement at all?"

You are the doctor, I wanted to say, you tell me. I had been coming to his office twice a week for a month, sitting in the gloom, staring at the muddle on his desk, answering his foolish questions, to the best of my ability, and paying fifteen dollars an hour for the pleasure. I had had enough.

"A little," I lied.

He leaned back in the big chair that made him look smaller and unbuttoned the jacket of another of his dapper suits. The dim light from the lamp on his desk glinted off the gold chain strung across his vest. As he rocked back and forth, the reflection went on and off.

"There is something I can give you . . ." he began.

I could not believe my ears. The man was a fool. Worse than that, a charlatan. He had wasted a month of my life asking about things that had nothing to do with my voice when all he had to do was prescribe some medication, and I would be able to speak again. I could have picked up *The Burghers of Calais* and crowned him. But I managed to keep my voice calm. I had made a considerable amount of money since the day I had sat for the psychological examination in the former SS office, but anger was still a luxury beyond my means.

"What are we waiting for?" I asked.

"It's a simple procedure. I administer a small dose of sodium amytal. While under the influence, you will be able to speak normally. You will also begin to recall events leading up to the loss of your voice."

"You mean truth serum?"

"An unfortunate term."

Unfortunate, Doctor, but accurate. Bloody accurate. You want to inject something into my veins that will start me talking.

"There's nothing to be afraid of," he said.

How in hell would you know?

"The treatment has proved effective with cases like yours."

Cases like mine? There are no cases like mine, Doctor, or only a handful. That is what you cannot get through your goddamn patent-leather head. I am not one of the millions who went in. I am one of the few who came out. How do you explain that? How do you justify that?

I took a handkerchief from my pocket to wipe the mustache of sweat that was gathering. I pushed my chair back a few inches. I needed room to stretch my legs. He was still watching me with that owlish stare, but I could not look at him. My glance ricocheted around the room, searching for something to hang on to. I felt the nooses on the Burghers of Calais tightening around my neck. That was when I saw it. It was lying on top of a low bookcase behind his desk. I cannot imagine how I had missed it before, but then I do not understand how I blotted it out the night Madeleine picked up a book from the bedside table, and I lost my voice. It was the same book. I was sure of it, though I could not fathom how it existed at all.

The dust jacket was a rusty red, the color of dried blood. Her photograph covered half the front. The huge eyes stared up at me. They were black with accusation. The full mouth was set. In what? In judgment. The face was small, the shoulders narrow and impossibly fragile. I had forgotten that she was a child. She would never be anything else.

How could this be? She died. They all died, all except Otto. I knew that from the Red Cross lists. I was the only one of whom there was no record.

Her name ran beneath the photograph. Bold white letters set in a black box straight and narrow as a coffin.

ANNE FRANK

Below it, the title was printed in script.

The Diary of a Young Girl

She is sitting at the small desk in her room scribbling. Dr. Pfeffer wants to use it, but she pleads for more time. She is hunched over the kitchen table making an entry. Mammichen is teasing her. Let me see it, Anne, just a page. She is curled in a chair, writing furiously in the notebook on her lap. Margot is in another chair, writing in her own diary. They are writing for posterity, as Mr. Bolkestein, the cabinet minister, has asked them to on the Dutch broadcast from London. After the war, he promises, a collection will be made of diaries and letters to show the world what life here was like. I will be published, Anne says, I will be famous. Margot makes no predictions about the future of her diary, though hers, we all assume, would be the one to attract attention. Margot is the serious sister.

But it is Anne's diary that the pig from the Grune Polizei dumps on the floor that warm summer morning they come to get us. Did a neighbor see a shadow behind a window shade? Did one of the men who worked below hear a sound, despite the stealth with which we moved during the day? Did a trades-man suspect the quantity of food Miep, formerly Otto's secre-tary, now our lifeline to the world, managed to scavenge, thanks to forged ration cards, and winning smiles, and the arrangement my father made with the butcher before we went into hiding? Someone must have tipped off the Green Police, because they know where to go. They mount the stairs with guns drawn, pull aside the bookcase that hides the entrance to the annex, and climb another flight to the cramped rooms. They wear civilian clothes, except for one who is in uniform. He asks where we keep our valuables. His fat fist closes around a wad of guilders. He eyes the jewelry, but cannot pick it up without dropping the money. He looks around for something to stuff his take in, grabs the briefcase with one hand, and upends it. Anne's notebooks tumble to the floor. Pages flutter after them. They twirl and see-saw and sail through a shaft of honeyed light that slants through one of the windows. None of us, not even Anne, glances at them as we leave the annex and walk out into that golden light for the first time in more than two years. A moment later the darkness of the police wagon closes around us.

"I think it's worth trying," Dr. Gabor said.

"There is no need." My words shook the walls of the small office.

Dr. Gabor sat up with a start. He had never heard my true voice before.

AS SOON as I got home that night, even before I climbed the stairs to tell Madeleine I had regained my voice, I went to the shelves in the family room. It took me some time to find the book. I went back and forth, my head bent to one side reading the spines, stooping to the bottom shelves, crooking my neck to see the top. Faulkner, Fitzgerald, Forster, Frank. I stopped. She had placed it among the fiction.

I took the book from the shelf, though I had no idea what I planned to do with it. Anne stared up at me. The eyes refused to blink. The eyes were indecent. I wanted to slide the lids closed. Instead, I reached up and put the book on the top shelf, beyond the grasp of my daughters, too high even for Madeleine.

"WHAT HAPPENED?" Madeleine kept asking.

"I have no idea," I kept telling her.

"Maybe it was something Dr. Gabor said," she suggested over dinner.

"Maybe," I agreed.

When I went down to the family room after dinner, the book was still on the top shelf where I had placed it. I could not keep from glancing at it as I moved about the room. I sensed it lurking behind me as we sat watching television. I heard the low murmur it gave off. Tell us the news, Peter. Tell us how the world goes on without us.

It was there when I came down the next morning, and when I returned home that evening, and the day after that. It was like an old friend or distant relative down on his luck, whom you take into the house with the best intentions, but grow to resent. And like that unwelcome guest, it followed me around, begging for notice, hungry for reassurance, desperate for something, though I could not say what.

It was keeping an eye on me that Saturday afternoon when Madeleine left me with the girls while she went shopping for a toaster to replace the one I had been unable to fix. That was something else. I was suddenly all thumbs around the house. Madeleine teased me about it. "If I had wanted someone who couldn't fix things, I would have found a Jewish husband." She came up behind me at my workbench, put her arms around my neck, and kissed the top of my head. She did not care about the toaster, but she was euphoric about the return of my voice. The loss of it had worried her more than she had let on.

I was sitting on the sofa in the family room the afternoon she went shopping, with one eye on the newspaper and the other on my daughters. Abigail was making me an imaginary cake on the small pink stove my mother-in-law had bought her for her birthday. Betsy was crooning a tale of wonder to a crowd of toys. My children's presence still astonished me. The awe was no less now than the night I had brought Abigail home from the hospital.

Madeleine had gone to sleep early that night. She was exhausted and would have to get up in a few hours to nurse the baby. But I went into the room that still smelled of fresh paint for one last look before I turned in. I had to see her again. I had to make sure she was still there.

I had planned to check on her and leave, but the sight of my daughter held me to the crib like a force of gravity. I stood staring down at her for several minutes. Finally, I pulled the rocking chair up to the crib, sat, and snaked my arm between the slats. Was her skin supposed to be this hot? She pulled her tiny legs to her chest. She smacked her lips. Her hand closed around my finger. She might as well have turned a key in the lock of the nursery door. I could not leave the room. I could not even withdraw my finger. Even after her fist relaxed, I was still a prisoner. This small piece of humanity, this living thing, was made of the same matter as I. I had not been able to get over the miracle. I still could not. Betsy's arrival only intensified the experience. I was connected.

As I sat with one eye trained on my daughters that afternoon, a movement on the top shelf caught my attention. The book seemed to be vibrating.

I sat watching it, pinned to my seat, helpless to move. It gyrated back and forth. It teetered on the edge. It began to fall. The distance between the top shelf and the floor stretched. The book picked up speed and force. It was no good telling myself I was imagining things. The book kept coming. It was a boulder about to crash, a meteorite heading straight for my children.

I freed myself from the grip of the sofa and sprang toward my daughters. Abigail's head snapped up, her face streaked with terror. Betsy began to shriek. I scooped them up, one in each arm, and held their surprisingly solid bodies to me. I looked up. The book was still on the top shelf.

I HAD to get it out of the house, but I could not think what to do with it. I could not burn it. That was what they had done to books. I would not throw it in the trash. That was what they had done to us.

On Monday morning, I took it from the shelf and carried it out to the car. I did not like driving around with it beside me on the front seat, my uninvited passenger, my unwelcome past, but I would figure out something to do with it.

It was still there when I came out of the office that evening. The big dark eyes stared up at me. I turned the book over. The back of the jacket was covered with small cramped writing. THIS IS A PAGE FROM THE DIARY OF ANNE FRANK. The Dutch words marched across the page like insects. I opened the glove compartment, shoved the book in, and slammed the door shut on it.

The idea came to me as I was driving past the railroad station. I made a sudden, reckless turn into the parking lot. I would not destroy it. I would pass it on to someone else.

A handful of empty cars were parked off to one side. The area closest to the tracks, where wives sat behind steering wheels filing their nails, or reading magazines, or telling children in the backseat to stop fighting, while they waited for their

returning husbands, was empty. There was no one on the platform. I was between trains.

I pulled into one of the spots close to the tracks, took the book
from the glove compartment, and got out of the car. I could not
help glancing around me, though there was nothing illegal about
leaving a book for some bored commuter or curious traveler to
pick up. I sprinted up the stairs to the platform. I felt lighter than
I had in days. By the time I reached the top of the steps, I was
weightless. That must have been why I did it. I cannot think of
any other reason. It was not what I had intended.

I was moving along at a brisk clip, with the book in my right
hand, but instead of heading for one of the benches, I veered
toward the tracks. Turning sideways, like a pitcher winding up
for the throw, I pulled my arm back, then circled it forward and
let the book fly. It soared over the tracks, weightless and free as
I was, hit the edge of the opposite platform with a smack, and
fell. I heard the thud as it struck the tracks. It lay between
them, spread-eagled across the ties.

I stood staring at it. I had not meant to destroy it. I had just
wanted to get it out of the house. I skulked back to the car, my
shoulders hunched, my head down. As I pulled out of the lot, a
car was turning into it. I averted my face.

WHEN I came into the family room twenty minutes later, my
eye went immediately to the top shelf. The slight gap between
the books was a gaping hole. The space grew wider as the night
wore on. I felt the emptiness like the physical hunger I had
thought would never go away.

It was after ten when I stood and told Madeleine that I had forgotten some papers at the office and had to drive over to get them.

"Why don't you just leave earlier in the morning?" There was no suspicion in her voice. I was a good husband, a loving father, a decent man, not the kind given to nocturnal wanderings. Everything I wanted was here in this house.

I told her I would be back in no time, went upstairs to get my car keys, and grabbed a flashlight on my way out the door. "To find the light switches in the building," I said before she could ask.

This time the lot was entirely empty. I parked next to the platform again. The opening and closing of the door sounded like someone groaning in the darkness.

I took the stairs two at a clip. I had no time to waste. I turned on the flashlight and raked the beam over the tracks. It took me several sweeps to find it, though it lay where it had landed on the ties between the tracks.

I walked to the edge of the platform. The drop to the tracks was not high. I jumped. My ankle turned as I hit the ground. My knees buckled. I regained my balance just before I fell.

I started across the tracks, following the beam of the flashlight. My shoes crunched on the gravel. The light bobbed and circled in the darkness. A shape skittered through it. Eyes glittered. A tail slithered. The scar from the rat bite on my arm throbbed, though it had never given me trouble in the past.

I was moving quickly, despite the pain in my ankle. There were few trains at this hour, and even if one came through, I would hear it in the distance and see the lights, but it was still not an intelligent thing to be doing, not for a husband and father, not for anyone.

Another rat slithered through the beam of light. I followed it with the flashlight until it burrowed into a hole beneath the platform. When I focused the light back on the track, the book was gone. I waved the flashlight around. The long white beam sliced and circled. Goddamn the rat. Goddamn the book. If it were not for that, I would be home, my wife reading at my side, my daughters sleeping across the hall. The flashlight swept up one track and down the other, skittered across the ties, climbed the sides of the platform, crept slowly back, and came to rest inches from where I stood. The black eyes stared up at me. Where have you been, Peter? I have been waiting for you.

I stooped to the book. The dirt and cinders felt gritty between my fingers as my hand curled around it. I started back across the tracks. The flashlight danced over the rails.

When I reached the platform, I placed the book and the light on the concrete to leave my arms free and put my hands, palms down, on the edge to give myself leverage. I bent my arms, then stiffened them and flung my legs up, but the platform was higher than I had thought. My knee hit the concrete. My legs buckled under me as I fell to the tracks. I imagined Betsy curled in her crib. I pictured Abigail in her bed, a downy arm holding a stuffed bear in a stranglehold. I saw Madeleine glance at the clock.

I bent my arms again, stiffened them again, flung my legs again, and fell back to the tracks again. It took three more attempts to heave myself onto the platform. My hands were scraped and bloody, and my knees and shins were sore from being beaten against the concrete. When I got back in the car, I saw that I had torn one leg of my trousers.

I put the book back in the glove compartment. It would be all right there, for the moment.

When I got home, Madeleine was sitting up in bed, reading. She lifted her eyes from the page, took in my bloody hands and torn trousers, and asked what on earth had happened. I told her I had tripped going down the stairs from the building to the parking lot. She asked what had happened to the flashlight I had taken. I said the battery had gone dead. As my lies went, this one was small change.

FOR THE next week I kept moving the book around. Just as others who had gone into hiding had stolen from cellars to closets to caves, when benefactors got frightened, or neighbors grew suspicious, or hush money ran out, so I kept finding new places for my charge. I took it from the glove compartment of my car and put it back on the shelf in the family room that was out of everyone's reach except my own. I hid it behind my workbench in the basement. I locked it in the safe at the back of the linen closet. The safe was not large, and there was barely room for the book with the passport and the manila folder of cash I kept there. I took it out of the safe. I did not want it contaminating the other things. I locked it in the top drawer of the desk in my office. I had no intention of reading it, but I could not abandon it.

Still, it followed me around. I had managed not to notice it when it had lain on the night table on the other side of the bed where I slept. The ads and reviews had escaped my attention, because I never looked at that section of the paper. But now that I knew about the book, it was inescapable. On the street, women carried it clutched to their breasts like badges of honor. Behind the cash register in the diner where Harry and I sometimes had lunch, the girl looked up from it accusingly when we interrupted her to pay our checks. Coming into my office one afternoon, I caught a glimpse of Anne's face before my secretary swept her back to her hiding place in the desk. I felt like a wanted man who sees posters for his arrest everywhere.

"You can't imagine what this means. The diary would come out in German and English, telling everything that went on in our lives when we were in hiding—all the fears, disputes, food, politics, the Jewish question, the weather, moods, problems of growing-up, birthdays and reminiscences—in short, everything."

—Otto Frank in a letter, November 11, 1945,
quoted in *The Hidden Life of Otto Frank,*
by Carol Ann Lee

"Though I have been beaten, I have no scars left."
—Otto Frank in a letter, January 26, 1975,
quoted in *The Hidden Life of Otto Frank,*
by Carol Ann Lee

SEVEN

■ ■ I HAD NOT PLANNED TO READ IT, but I finally did.
■ ■ How could I not? I read it at my workbench in the basement, when I was supposed to be building a toy chest for Abigail's room; and in the bathroom in the middle of the night, while Madeleine slept on the other side of the locked door; and in the parking lot of a supermarket where she did not shop because though the prices were lower, the produce was inferior; and in the railroad parking lot, until she asked one night if that had been my car she had seen as she drove past the station

that afternoon. Railroad stations worried her. Her sister had recounted the story of a survivor of one too many cattle cars, who had lain down on the tracks and waited for a train to go over him. The accident, if that is what you call it, halted trains going in both directions for hours. I told Madeleine it had not been my car, and stopped going there, but I did not stop reading the diary. I could not. I was like a boy with a secret vice, as I had been then, lying in the coffin-narrow bed, holding on to myself, not caring whether my parents on the other side of the damp sweating wall heard, or whether I went blind, or crazy, or grew hair on my palms, because I would probably be dead before any of that could happen.

When I was not reading it, I was thinking about it. Such, as Dr. Gabor might have pointed out had I continued to see him, is the nature of a secret vice. It became my real world, more real than the basement where I built things for my wife and children; than the bathroom where I tried to escape under a pounding shower, though why I should think I could escape those memories in a shower, of all places, I cannot imagine; than the supermarket parking lot where women hurried past with obscenely full shopping carts. The dampness of the canal crawling up the walls was real, and the stench of mildew and sweat and farts and piss and shit, and the taste of rotten potatoes and moldy beans, and the cold that turned my mother's hands white as frost under the moth-eaten gloves, and the heat that beat down from the sky and steamed up from the streets where we were forbidden to walk, and the terror, and the degradation of that terror. I was trapped in that book as I had been trapped in that house. But—and this was what I could not understand—I was homesick for it too. I longed for those rank-smelling rooms where the walls steamed in summer and dripped as if in a cold sweat in winter. I yearned for those parents. I missed Anne. I ached for myself.

Occasionally I grew angry. It was not only that she had changed the names, though that was bad enough. When she had called Pfeffer Dussel, which was German for idiot, behind his back in the annex, it was the innocent joke of two young people straining against the leash, but now poor Pfeffer was Dussel for the ages. She had also mauled and manhandled my mother and father. These renamed van Daans were not my parents, I wanted to shout at her, but I could not, because the aroma of my father's cigarettes closed my throat and the sound of my mother's laughter drowned out my voice. I was no match for the memories the diary brought back. I could not resist the pull of those ghosts. They rose from the torn gritty pages, threw their arms around my neck, and wrestled me panting and laughing and sobbing back into their lives, back into the time when they were alive.

My mother crooks a ringed finger. Remember the night I cut your hair? she whispers, and we are dancing around the room, I in my swimming shorts and tennis shoes, she in a mended print dress, my hands on her wrists, her arms thrashing in mock struggle. She is laughing and crying and screaming at me to leave her alone, and I am pushing and pulling and flinging her around the room, half in fun, half in fury, filled with terror at the power, which for a moment overwhelms the other terror, the one we all live with.

My father shouts at me to give him the book, not the book I am hunched over in the dusk-shrouded car, but another book, because I am too young to know about such things—though I am not too young to go with him and Mr. Frank down to the offices, my hand gripping the hammer in case we come upon the burglars—and he grabs that other book, the one about penises and vaginas and sexual intercourse, from my hands, and we shove and slap and kick, and he curses me and sends me to the attic without dinner, where I sit listening to the earthquake rumble of my empty stomach and the sounds of them eating and talking and rattling dishes below me, and wish him dead, though I know it is an unconscionable thought under the circumstances. He is a fool, I rant in my head, a bigger dussel than Pfeffer. At least Pfeffer got his son on the ship to England.

But then another time, we are kneeling, my father and I, shoulder to shoulder, as we fit the screens into the food safe we are building, and Mr. Frank, who helps me with my English but cannot build anything practical, stands watching. My father says quietly, as if it is a secret we must keep from the others who do not understand how to make things, well done, Peter, well done.

I sat in the supermarket parking lot, hearing my father murmuring in my ear, as I stared at the book propped up against the steering wheel. It was an invalid, its binding broken from being flung onto the railroad tracks, its pages torn from the fall. I reached over, opened the glove compartment, and took out a roll of Scotch tape. And just as I might bandage Abigail's knee or kiss Betsy's booboo, I began mending the book's wounds. I hummed as I worked. Madeleine says I often hum while I work, though I am not conscious of the fact. But suddenly I became aware of it. I was humming Mozart. *Eine kleine Nachtmusik* filled the car, and I am back in the front attic with Anne. It is the evening of Easter Sunday, the second Easter Sunday we spent there, the last we will spend there, and we are listening to the music on the radio, while the chestnut tree outside the window makes a spiteful promise of spring.

I finished my ministrations and began leafing through the book again.

It is my mother's birthday, and my father gives Miep money in hope she can find red carnations, his traditional gift. My mother screams with pleasure at the scarlet excitement in our gray lives, and throws her arms around my father's neck, and kisses him lingeringly on the mouth, but now instead of turning away in disgust, as I did then, I narrow my eyes to see them more clearly. How young they are; my mother buxom and bustling with a wide mouth ready to take a bite out of life; my father tall, dapper, wreathed in cigarette smoke and corny jokes. What goes click ninety-nine times and clack once? A centipede with a club foot. Do they love each other? Do they make love in this putrid unprivate annex?

I hear them screaming at each other.

"I won't sell the coat."

"Fine, we'll eat rabbit fur this winter."

"You only want the money to squander on your cigarettes."

"You want it to buy more clothes after the war. After the war! What do we eat until after the war?"

But they make up. They always make up. He steals up behind her as she stands at the sink, reaches around her, and cups her melon breasts in his big nicotine-stained hands. "Don't," she shrieks, and the word becomes yes in her mouth. "Kerli," he croons into her ear. And they waltz into the bedroom.

Greedy, Anne calls them. Oh, yes, they are greedy.

I keep turning the pages, hungry for news of us. An entry stops me.

Peter's very shy, but not too shy to admit that he'd be perfectly happy not to see his parents for a year or two.

I am staggering around the annex, bouncing from one damp crumbling wall to another. I am suffocating here, too big for the low ceilings and cramped rooms, too strong for my terrified helpless mother and raging powerless father, too old to be beaten down by her and beaten by him. My huge feet make too much noise. My long arms knock things over. I fear I will smash them all. I dream of smashing them all.

I reached out and picked up a pack of cigarettes Harry had left on the front seat. Holding the book with one hand, I shook out a cigarette and pushed in the lighter. I did not even know what I was doing until I inhaled. The smell of my father closed around me. I could barely breath. I wrenched open the car door to get some air. The book tumbled out of my lap onto the ground. Anne stared up at me from the black tar of the parking lot. I picked her up, brushed her off, closed the car door. Her steady eyes gazed at me from her eternally childish face.

"The grown-ups are just jealous because we're young," I whisper, as we climb the stairs from my bedroom to the attic.

But they are younger than we, or at least more innocent. Outside the annex, bombs fall, and murderers march the streets, and freight cars carry their cargo east, while inside, the parents, who never see eye to eye on anything, agree that Anne and I should not spend evenings together alone in the dark, and Otto, who still trusts in the old decencies—I was an officer in the German army in the last war, he will tell the man from the Grune Polizei, as the brute stuffs our valuables into the briefcase—takes me aside and speaks of primrose paths, and one thing leading to another, and saving ourselves, or at least Anne, for the future. What future? I want to ask him, but I do not, because I need to believe he is right. Nonetheless, Anne and I continue to climb the stairs to the attic, where we sit in the darkness, inhaling the first ripe stirrings of spring and the rank fumes rising from the canal in front of the house, and holding on to each other for dear life. If God lets her live, she says under cover of night, she will achieve more than her mother ever did, and make her voice heard, and work for mankind. If I survive, I tell her, I will go to the Dutch East Indies and make something of myself. But gradually we stop talking and begin, with halting steps, to find our way down Otto's primrose path. I feel her childish body coming of age within my arms, and life shrieks in my ears, or maybe only the air-raid sirens.

I close my eyes, but Anne and my father and mother, and all of them, even poor Pfeffer, are imprinted on the inside of my lids. There is no getting away from them. I open my eyes. Drops of water spatter Anne's face on the dust jacket of the book. It has begun to rain. I reach out to roll up the window. It is already closed. I look up. The sun hangs like a tarnished coin above the supermarket.

I take a handkerchief from my pocket, blow my nose, and look around. Women hurry past, their bodies cantilevered forward with the effort of pushing their overflowing baskets, their eyes cutting to me, then away. A boy stops to stare. His mother grabs his hand and drags him away. Another woman does not even take the chance. Holding a child with one hand, she steers her cart in a wide circle around me. I stare out at them from the cage of my car. I read their suspicions as clearly as if they hang over their heads in ballooned captions. Madman. Criminal. Murderer.

■   ■   ■   ■

THAT NIGHT, as Madeleine slept beside me, I got out of bed and padded quietly down to the kitchen. After the soft carpeting, the linoleum felt cold and slippery beneath my bare feet. I closed the louvered doors before I switched on the overhead light and blinked against the brilliance. On the way to the refrigerator, I leaned against the window, cupping my eyes with my hands to shut out the glare of the room, and looked out at my neighbors' houses. A full moon spilled a ghostly glow over the yards, but no lights burned. Indian Hills slept, peacefully, I imagined.

I crossed to the refrigerator, opened the door, and began taking things out. One after another, I carried them to the table. Two chicken legs, a slab of meatloaf, half a pie, a jar of peanut butter, a bottle of milk, a bowl of spaghetti covered with waxed paper, a half-eaten jar of baby food. I had worked my way through one chicken leg and the spaghetti, when Madeleine pushed open the louvered doors. She blinked against the lights. Her eyes moved from plate to bowl to bottle of my obscene banquet, then to me.

"Are you all right?" she asked gently.

"Just a little hungry."

Her eyes lighted on the jar of baby food.

"I must have been half asleep." I stood and carried the baby food back to the refrigerator. "I thought it was regular applesauce."

She was still staring at me when I turned back from the refrigerator, her lovely loving face screwed into a knot of worry. My poor wife was beginning to suspect what I had known all along. She had not won such a prize after all.

"He [Peter] said life would have been much easier if he'd been a Christian or could become one after the war. I asked if he wanted to be baptized, but that wasn't what he meant either. He said he'd never be able to feel like a Christian."

—*The Diary of a Young Girl,*
by Anne Frank, February 16, 1944

EIGHT

■ ■ I THOUGHT OF GOING BACK to Amsterdam, just for a
■ ■ week or two. I told myself I would put the ghosts to
rest. What I really wanted was to bring them back to life. I lay
in bed at three in the morning, that treacherous hour when
everything comes crawling back, hearing my mother threaten
suicide because she is so afraid of dying; and my father rage
because we have no money left to give Miep to buy us food; and
me apologize for forgetting to unbolt the door to the street. At
night, after the workers are gone, we creep out of the cramped
annex down to the offices and warehouse on the lower floors.
For a few hours, we have the run of the building, but we always

lock the door to the street to be safe. It is my job to unlock it before we go back into hiding, but that night I forget, and the next morning the men cannot get in. I lay in bed now, swearing I would return. I would unbolt the door. I would right the wrongs. I would save them.

But when dawn streaked the windows, I knew I would not go back. I could not return to that world. Miep, and her husband Jan, and Kleiman, and Kugler had risked their lives to save ours, but there were others. I remembered the words some good Dutch citizen had scrawled on the bridge across the canal from the windows we were not supposed to look out of. *Keep your dirty hands off our dirty Jews.* From what I had heard in the DP camp, things were no better since the war. People came home from the camps to find neighbors sleeping in their beds, and eating at their tables, and forgetting they had ever known them, let alone agreed to take care of their cherished possessions until they could reclaim them. Haven't you caused enough trouble? the good people of Amsterdam asked. We had our own hardship, they insisted. If they killed so many in the camps, they wanted to know, how come so many are returning? German Jews had the worst of both worlds. The Dutch government rescinded the Nazi laws against Jews, then designated German Jews enemy nationals. I would not go back to that, even as a gentile.

It came to me in another three-A.M. wide-awake nightmare. I would go to church. I would embrace my new self more fully.

I had my pick of Episcopalian and Presbyterian and Lutheran and Catholic and probably half a dozen others I had not even noticed in my travels about the area. Madeleine would think it strange. Neither of us believed. We had agreed to raise the children without superstition. But she had seen me return from a trip to the office looking as if I had been worked over by a handful of hoodlums, and stumbled upon me taking food out of the baby's mouth, and spotted my car lurking in the station parking lot, though I had denied that. Surely she could take an uncharacteristic visit to church in her stride.

I cruised past Christ Church, which was only a few minutes from the house, but did not stop. I parked in front of St. Michael's, but the statue of Jesus on the cross, where I, if the taunts of my youth were to be believed, had put him, warned me away. When I noticed a police car approaching in the rearview mirror, as I sat in front of All Souls, I turned the key in the ignition, threw the gearshift into first, and almost collided with another car in my haste to get away.

IT WAS barely light when I backed the car down the driveway the next morning. Madeleine was still asleep. I had kissed her tangled hair and whispered that I had an early meeting I had forgotten to mention.

"Don't wake the baby," she murmured and burrowed into another few minutes of sweet unconsciousness.

A slick of fallen leaves turned the driveway treacherous beneath the tires. When I reached the highway, I glanced down at the speedometer. I was going fifteen miles above the speed limit. I did not brake. I put the dun-colored marshes and hulking oil tanks of New Jersey behind me, crossed the Goethals Bridge, and kept going east. I had not been back in years, but I still knew the way. When I had passed the building in those days, I had always quickened my step to get by as fast as possible.

I found a parking space a little way down the block. The rain had turned to mist. It rose from the street carrying the ripe rank smell of the sewers. A man walked a three-legged dog. Two boys splashed through a puddle. A woman, bundled into a raincoat and kerchief, made her way around it. None of them so much as glanced at me. Doors turned suspicious faces to the street. Mind-your-own-business hung in the wet morning air. I was a long way from Indian Hills.

The red brick façade, streaked black by the rain, needed pointing, and a sheet of cardboard covered a hole in one window. The heavy wooden door gave easily, though from the look of it, I had thought it would stick. The smell of old books and camphor and cabbage assailed me. I did not understand the cabbage.

From where I stood, I could look down a narrow aisle to the front of the synagogue. It ran past rows of pews, separated about a third of the way down by a dusty purple curtain. I had forgotten the curtain. On Friday nights and Saturdays and holidays, it would be drawn across to separate the men from the women.

I started down the aisle, past the curtain, toward the front of the long narrow room. The ark stood open. The Torah lay on a tall wooden table. A group of men, swathed in prayer shawls, huddled around it, chanting. Though I did not understand the words, something in me responded to the inconsolable cadence, but what soul does not keen to a minor-key dirge? As they chanted, they bent their knees, then straightened to pitch their bodies forward. The motion too was familiar, though I had never emulated it. The thought that it might be in my blood chilled me. That would prove *them* right. But was that not why I was here?

One of the men detached himself from the group and began backing up the aisle toward me, dipping and bobbing and chanting as he came. When he reached me and turned, I was surprised. From a distance, wrapped in their prayer shawls, crowned with skullcaps, they all looked old, but this man was about my age. His black cap sat jauntily on a mass of wiry carrot-colored hair. Beneath leather straps that bound a small black box to his forehead, rusty freckles sprinkled his milky skin. The hair, it occurred to me, would have saved him, if it didn't kill him first. They would have done experiments, in the interest of science, to find out about this minor curiosity, a redheaded Jew. He dipped again. I was not sure whether it was part of the dance or if he was bowing to me. He held a black-bound book out to me. As he did, his prayer shawl fell away. Straps binding another black leather box to his arm dug into the flesh and distorted the tattooed number. He went on holding the book out to me, just as the customs officer on the pier that morning had held out my papers. I took it from him.

He nudged me into the pew and followed. Though he was holding an open book in one hand, he did not look at it. As he went on praying, he kept his eyes on me. I focused mine straight ahead. He reached over, flipped open the book I was holding, rifled through it, then looked at me and nodded toward the open pages. I looked down at it. Strange characters scuttled across the surface. I recognized the shapes, but I did not comprehend the meaning. I did not even know the sounds they signified. I lifted my eyes to the open ark. My gaze rose, but my spirit did not follow. I felt nothing. I closed my eyes and concentrated on the lament of the praying men. I bent my knees and tried to pitch my shoulders forward, but something strong as a steel wire from the heavens held me straight. I waited for a reaction. I wanted my stomach to churn with hunger. I hoped the hairs would stand up on the back of my neck. But it was no good. The sight of Anne's diary had stricken me mute. These half-recollected objects and rituals did not even give me goose bumps.

I waited until the worshippers shouted their last amens and began taking off their prayer shawls, then started up the aisle. The man with the red hair followed me, as I knew he would. He caught up as I reached the door and leaned close to say something. I caught a powerful whiff of mothballs. Mothball cookies, Anne called them as my mother took them out of the tin, because they had been stored in a mothproofed closet. Standing in that alien synagogue, I could taste the sweet stickiness melting on my tongue.

"You're a Jew?" he asked.

I stood staring at the old-looking young man. His hair stood out on his head as if an electric current had run through it. His threadbare sleeveless sweater bagged over a frayed flannel shirt, his dusty trousers drooped onto scuffed shoes.

"I am an American," I said.

"Me also. I was anything else, you think I could be standing here in shul? Downtown Warsaw, I wouldn't have it so good. Germany, I wouldn't even talk about. I know you're an American, Mr. Yankee Doodle Dandy, but are you a Jew?"

I did not answer him.

"It's a simple question. Like the song says, is you is or is you ain't?"

I had not told my wife, or her sister before her, or my partner. I would never tell my children. I had done it partly for them. So why should I tell this stranger, this greenie who was sticking to me like a fly to paper?

"I am."

He nodded.

"But not a believer."

He parted his thin lips in a feral smile. "About believing, I didn't ask." He leaned closer. I caught the scent of mothballs again and tasted the cookies. "So tell me, you'll be back? Men like you, we need."

"Men like me?"

"A minyan."

For a moment I thought he said minion. I was going to tell him I was not that. Then another word I had forgotten came back. He wanted me to make up a minyan, the quorum of ten men required for prayer.

I told him I would be back, though I was sure I would not.

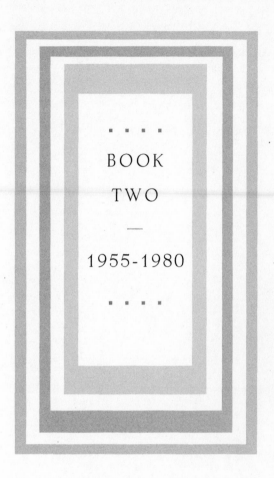

. . . .

BOOK

TWO

—

1955-1980

. . . .

"I'll never forget the time in Auschwitz when the seventeen-year-old Peter van Pels and I saw a group of selected men. Among those men was Peter's father. The men marched away. Two hours later a truck came by loaded with their clothing."

—Otto Frank,
quoted in *Anne Frank Magazine*, 1998

"[T]he Frank and Van Pels* families and Friedrich Pfeffer [arrived] at the station [in Auschwitz] on the night of September 5-6. . . . Their 'selection' took place on the platform . . . 549 persons—among them all the children under the age of fifteen—were gassed that same day, September 6. Among them was [Hermann] Van Pels."

—*The Diary of Anne Frank:
The Critical Edition*, based on the
Netherlands Red Cross dossier 103586

NINE

■ ■ THIS DOCTOR'S NAME WAS MILLER. Dr. Joseph Miller. ■ ■ He looked just as ordinary as he sounded. That was fine with me. I wanted no more Gabors, mining Old World memories, reeking of Old World miseries. I had not come here because anything was wrong. This time I had made an appoint-

*When the Critical Edition of the diary was published in 1989, the real names of the characters, rather than the names Anne made up, were used in the explanatory essays.

ment with a doctor because everything was going so well. My voice was fine. I never even thought about the incident anymore. The diary had thrown me at first, only because I had assumed it had gone up in smoke, like everything else. The idea of its living in the wake of all that death was somehow obscene. But I had managed to put it in perspective. It was only a book. Even when I read that there would be a play made from it, I was not upset. If that was what Otto wanted, who was I to object? I felt sorry for him, all that living in the past, but it was no skin off my nose.

I had a wife, whom I loved, and who loved me in return; two healthy daughters; and another child on the way. Three months earlier, Madeleine had announced, as I walked in the door one evening, that the rabbit had died. The words were a code, but I understood them immediately. Every husband in Indian Hills knew what they meant, probably every husband in America. I wondered if any of them, other than me, found it peculiar that we used the language of death to announce the coming of life. I did not say that to my wife. I did what all the husbands up and down Seminole Road, throughout Indian Hills, across America, would do under the circumstances, all, that is, except the philanderers and drunks and non-family-men. I crossed the kitchen, took her in my arms, kissed her, and told her how pleased I was. I went through all the proper motions. I do not mean to imply that I was merely going through the motions. My joy was genuine. But I am not given to effusive behavior. If I had made a fuss, Madeleine would have worried that something was wrong.

She was hoping for a boy, not only because we had two girls, but because she was sure that I, like every man, she thought, wanted a son. She was wrong about that. Much as I would have liked a son, I was hoping for another daughter. A girl would let me off the hook.

Business was going well too. Harry had been right about every Joe and his wife wanting a brand-new house in the suburbs. We had broken ground for the third extension of the development. The National Association of Home Builders had even given us an award. At first I had been reluctant to accept it. I did not like the idea of calling attention to myself.

Harry rolled his eyes at the office ceiling when I told him that. "People pay good money to press agents to get their names in the paper, and my partner doesn't like calling attention to himself."

He was right. This fear of standing out was the last vestige of my greenie mentality. As long as I thought that way, I might as well be back at the Marseilles. The award could do nothing but good. I even let him talk me into giving the acceptance speech at the luncheon, though I thought he should be the one to do it.

"I have an accent," I said.

"So do I. Pure Brooklynese. Face it, pal, you're the reason we're getting this cockamamie award. We build a nice little house, but so do a lot of other guys. They're even catching on about the bigger rooms at the same cost. There's only one difference between us and them. You. Peter van Pels. Living proof that America is still the land of opportunity. That anybody can bubble to the top of the melting pot. Of course, it doesn't hurt if he's not a member of the tribe." He winked.

I gave the acceptance speech at the lunch. Afterward, men came up to me, and shook my hand, and offered me their cards. A photographer took pictures. The local newspaper ran an article with a photograph. The *Journal American* printed a paragraph. Madeleine had it propped up on the counter when I arrived home that evening.

"Take a look at that." She nodded toward the newspaper, then pushed a curl from her forehead with the back of her hand. When she first sheared off her hair in something called a poodle cut, I hated it. I prefer long hair on women. The predilection is understandable. But I had grown accustomed to this girlish hairdo. It was named after a dog, but it lent a feline cast to her long eyes and sharply boned cheeks. She seemed at once watchful and content, though that might have been the pregnancy.

"What is it?"

"An article on my famous husband."

"In a New York paper?" This was more than I had bargained for. Surely someone would see it, though I could not imagine who.

I picked up the paper, skimmed the article once, then read it through a second time more slowly. It was an innocuous paragraph about an ordinary American businessman. Only a greenie would be afraid of it.

Madeleine bought three copies each of the *Journal American* and the local paper, clipped the articles, and had them laminated. She gave one set to her mother and another to her sister. I was not there when she handed them over, but I can see her smiling, sleek and smug as if she were licking the milk from her whiskers. Though no one would admit it, the family kept score. Norman had gone to college and medical school, but I had read Goethe and Schiller "in the original." He was a professional man, but I made more money. The first person Madeleine called when she found out about the award was her father. My father-in-law admired my brother-in-law's credentials, Norman Fine, M.D., F.A.C.P., but he liked what he called my gumption. He was in awe of Norman's intimacy with issues of life and death, but a little disdainful of Norman's ignorance of hardship. He loved me, he occasionally said, like a son, even if I was a shagetz. Have I mentioned that my father-in-law was a self-made man?

The award made me wish I could tell my own father, though I seldom thought of him or my mother these days. What was there to think of? They were gone. That part of my life was dead and buried.

I believed in the future. That was why I was in Dr. Joseph Miller's office, that and my daughter Abigail. Abigail was six now, old enough for shame. That was the expression I had seen on her face when I looked up from my workbench in the basement one afternoon.

I was putting the finishing touches on the dollhouse I had built for her. Susannah's daughter Debbie was with us. Debbie was five months older than Abigail and, in my daughter's wide blue-gray eyes, the source of all wisdom and sound judgment. I thought my niece had a streak of sadism, but perhaps I was an overprotective father. That was the term Madeleine used.

I was hanging the last roll of flocked wallpaper in the tiny Victorian dining room. It was delicate work, especially for hands as big as mine, and I was hunched over, peering into the house, concentrating on the job at hand. The two girls were standing at the side of the workbench watching me. They had been chattering and giggling and whispering all afternoon, and at first I did not notice the silence. It was only when I smoothed the paper on the wall and leaned back that I saw they were staring at me. No, not at me, at my left arm. Debbie's mouth was a small rosebud of revulsion. But it was my daughter's expression that cut. I recognized it immediately, though I had not seen it in years. It was the expression we had worn, not when we were subjected to horror ourselves, but when we were forced to witness it being perpetrated on others. It was shame. And it had no place on my daughter's face.

The next morning I called to make an appointment with Dr. Miller. I had been putting it off for months, perhaps years, but now I was ready.

"It's a simple procedure," the doctor told me as he leaned back in his chair, which, come to think of it, was not unlike Gabor's big tip-and-swivel model, but there the similarity ended. Miller's crew cut, sparse and yellow as the down on a baby chick, gave him an air of improbable naïveté. No grown man could be that innocent. His starched white jacket looked sterile. His eyes, behind heavy horn-rimmed glasses, focused an inch above my head. Maybe that was the secret of his innocence. He did not look at his fellow man too closely.

"What we do, Mr. van Pels, is excise the number, as we would a tumor or mole. Then we advance the edges of the undermined skin to a close. If the area is too large for that, we graft skin, but I'm sure that won't be necessary in your case. Yours is just an ordinary garden-variety tattoo."

An ordinary, garden-variety tattoo, like millions of others. At least there had been millions of others at one time. These days there were fewer of them around, and not because of Dr. Miller and his colleagues. But I was not going to think about that. The fact that others had died with theirs did not mean I had to live with mine. More to the point, it did not mean my daughter had to live with mine.

"If you decide to go ahead with this—"

"I have already decided."

"Good." The doctor stood. "My girl will schedule an appointment." He came around the desk to where I was standing and began moving toward the door. "There's no reason to walk around with an unsightly blemish like that in this day and age." A blemish. I had never thought of it that way. "You'd be amazed the advances we've made. I'm not saying we can play God." He ran his hand over the yellow fuzz on his head. "But we can undo a lot of nature's mistakes. Man's too. I've removed dozens of numbers just like yours."

There were no numbers just like mine. That was the point. The numbers were the only individuality they had left us. One after another we stepped up to the table, Mr. Frank, Dr. Pfeffer, my father, I, and presented our arms, as directed. We were lucky. We understood German. Those who did not, those who had no idea what they were supposed to do, were kicked and beaten and worse. But we were only numbered, that day, consecutive numbers. Mine differed from my father's by only one digit. My indelible legacy.

"That's modern plastic surgery for you," Dr. Miller said as he opened the door and stepped aside to let me leave. "We erase the past."

I FELT him sitting beside me in the car on the way home, his left arm resting on the maroon leather upholstery of the front seat. The soot-dark number, identical to mine except for that last digit, throbbed against flesh that was pasty from two years without sunlight

I reached out and turned on the car radio. Ike was recovering nicely from his coronary thrombosis, and Roy Campanella had hit a first-inning two-run homer, resuscitating hope that the Dodgers might finally win a World Series title, and several thousand people had attended a Carnegie Hall rally to free Morton Sobell, who was serving twenty years for his part in the Julius and Ethel Rosenberg spy case. The Rosenbergs had gone to the electric chair more than two years ago, and still a month did not go by without some organization swearing to right old wrongs. People should know better. You cannot right old wrongs. Still, it was a sorry affair, this electrocuting of an ordinary couple, a mother and father, Jews, as my father-in-law always pointed out, as if their religious affiliation were responsible not only for their predicament, but for his shame. You cannot have it both ways, I wanted to tell him. If they are innocent scapegoats, you cannot be guilty by association.

You know who I blame for the Rosenberg business, though? Julius and Ethel. Not for spying. I cannot tell you whether they did or not. I blame them for going to the electric chair. I blame them for orphaning those two little boys. I can still see the newspaper photo of them in their plaid jackets and peaked caps. Michael and Robert. Good American names. Michael and Robert Rosenberg are smiling in the picture. The defense lawyer is leading them out of Sing Sing, it is probably the last time they will see their parents, and those poor unsuspecting boys are smiling. They have no idea what is in store for them. But I can tell them. I see them walking in that picture, the older one with an arm around his brother's shoulder, and I can predict it all. I feel the rough wool of the plaid jacket chafing against my neck and wrists. I see the oily black sheen of the guards' guns glinting in the sun. I hear the screams for mercy, for salvation, for some act of interference. No matter that the papers said the parents went to their deaths with silent dignity. What do newspapers know of such things? Those two little boys will hear their parents' cries for the rest of their lives. That is why I blame Julius and Ethel Rosenberg. They could have stopped the executions at any time. A telephone line was open to Washington till the last moment. All they had to do was confess, and their sentences would have been commuted to time in prison. Those two little boys could have gone on visiting them. By the time they became men, by the time they were my age, their parents might have been paroled. Most people are not so lucky. Most people do not get the chance to save themselves, or their families.

I switched off the radio. The Rosenbergs had nothing to do with me. I was not even tarnished by religious association, as my father-in-law seemed to think he was, though I admit old habits die hard. My instinct still divided the world into Jew and gentile. The only difference was that now I was on the safe side of the line.

I turned onto Seminole Road. These days I no longer expected to see smoking ruins or woods where no building had ever stood. I assumed the house would be there, freshly painted, with clean gutters and tended shrubbery, almost shaded by the trees that were growing up around it nearly as fast as my daughters. I no longer drove with both feet either. Sometimes I even took one hand off the wheel. And in a few weeks I would have no number, not even a scar, Dr. Miller had promised, as he gazed into the space above my head.

■   ■   ■   ■

I DID NOT tell Madeleine about the appointment with Dr. Miller. What was the point of worrying her ahead of time? Besides, I knew she would be relieved. There had been a time when she had been afraid to touch the tattoo. Even when we made love, she managed to avoid it. These days she was no longer squeamish about it, but that did not mean she would be sorry to have it gone. What kind of person would want to hold on to something like that? She would never say as much. She was too in awe of my past to suggest tinkering with it. She was too softhearted to risk wounding me. But I was doing this for all of us.

I waited until the night before I was to have the procedure to mention it to her. The doctor had said I would have to have someone drive me home. I told him I could do it myself, but he just smiled his untroubled smile and said he was the doctor. I disliked Miller's ingenuousness as much as I had Gabor's deviousness.

We were getting ready for bed when I brought the subject up. I did not want to mention it in front of the girls. They would notice the bandage, but once the dressing came off, they would forget the number had ever been there. Children have short memories. So do some adults, fortunately.

"I went to the doctor." I was untying my shoes, and kept my face down as I spoke. This was a statement, not an invitation to a discussion.

"Are you all right?" Her voice climbed half an octave in alarm.

"I'm fine. This is elective surgery."

I felt her behind me, standing on the other side of the bed, waiting. In her place, I would have known what was coming, but then I could never be in her place, any more than she could be in mine.

"I'm going to have the number removed. The one on my arm," I said, as if there were any other.

She did not answer immediately, but I knew what was going through her mind. She was glad to see it gone, but she could not admit she was glad, because that would be confessing it disgusted her.

"Is it dangerous?" she asked finally.

So I had been right.

"A piece of cake." The expression was Harry's, and the jaunty sound of it seemed appropriate to the occasion.

I looked up in time to see her straightening from stepping out of her slacks. Her belly strained against virginal white cotton panties. The skin above them was stretched thin and as pale as parchment, a shock next to her tawny arms and legs.

"The doctor does it in his office. With a local anesthetic."

"You're sure you want to do this?"

"I've made up my mind."

"When?"

"Two weeks ago."

"I mean when are you going to have it done?"

I stood and carried my shoes to the walk-in closet. "First thing tomorrow morning."

"Tomorrow morning!" The words were muffled by the door that hid me from her view.

"If I told you sooner," I called from inside the closet, "you'd only worry. I hadn't even planned to mention it until after it was over, but the doctor says I have to have someone to drive me home."

"I just wish you'd given me some warning. What would I have done if it weren't one of Mrs. Goralski's days?"

Mrs. Goralski came in three days a week to clean the house, and do the laundry, and stay with the girls, while Madeleine went to her meetings for good causes, and shopped with her mother and sister, and occasionally dressed up and took the train into New York to go to a museum or a matinee. She always said she felt guilty spending an afternoon playing while I worked so hard, but I did not begrudge her her fun. I was glad I could make it possible.

"But it is one of Mrs. Goralski's days," I said. "That's why I made the appointment."

I came out of the closet with a smile of assurance, but she missed it because she was lifting her nightgown over her head. I caught a flash of honeyed limbs and pale-moon flesh and dark pubic hair before it descended.

In the beginning of our marriage I had been afraid to look at my wife's body. Surely I would be punished for such pleasure. I was still in awe of it. My wonder had to do with the swell of pregnancy, but it was more than that. I marveled at the smoothness and wholeness of her. She was so perfectly intact. She had not even pierced her ears, as her mother and sister had. As I stood in the lingering glare of that momentary glimpse of her nakedness, I thought again how much better it would be if the child she was carrying was a girl.

■   ■   ■   ■   ■

MADELEINE AND I were alone in the waiting room, except for the receptionist, who was what Harry would call a knockout. I looked at my watch. The knockout had told us the doctor would be right with us. That was ten minutes ago.

"If he makes an appointment for ten o'clock, he ought to keep an appointment at ten o'clock," I muttered to Madeleine.

She looked up from her book, glanced at the receptionist, then leaned toward me. "It's only a little after ten," she whispered.

"Ten o'clock does not mean a little after ten. Where would I be if I kept people cooling their heels in my office?"

"You're just nervous."

"I'm not nervous. I just don't like being kept waiting."

"Maybe he had an emergency."

"Or maybe he likes to keep people waiting. He probably books more than one patient at a time. That's the way these doctors make money."

Madeleine caught my eye, then nodded toward the receptionist to warn me we could be overheard.

"Well, it is."

She repeated that I was nervous. I told her to stop saying that. There was nothing to be nervous about.

The door to the inner office opened. Another knockout, this one a little less pretty but with a better shape, or maybe it was only the effect of the white angel-of-mercy uniform, glanced around the room. Had she expected a crowd? Her eyes settled on me. "Mr. van Pels?"

I stood. Madeleine did too.

"Wait here," I said.

"Wouldn't you like moral support?"

I told her I would be fine.

"Just until he starts."

"Stay."

She looked stung, then remembered the two knockouts. My wife has her pride. She also prides herself on her sense of humor, especially in difficult situations. "Arf," she said, and looked from one to the other of them with a knowing, maternal, all-men-are-just-little-boys-at-heart smile, though she must have known there was little of the little boy left in me.

I crossed the office and started down the corridor behind the angel of mercy. She led me to a small room at the end of the hall, handed me a white gown, and told me to take off everything above the waist and put on the gown. "The doctor will be right with you."

I took off my jacket and tie and shirt and undershirt, hung them on a hanger on the back of the door, and put on the gown. There was a straight-backed chair in the corner. There was also a long table covered with a white sheet. I did not want to sit on that. I took the chair. I looked at my watch. It was 10:25. If I had not already taken off half my clothing, I would have left. I was not nervous, as Madeleine insisted. I was not having second thoughts. I simply did not like to be kept waiting. I would tell him so when he arrived.

The door opened. The doctor came in. The nurse followed him like a white sail in the wind of his importance. He did not apologize for being late. I did not mention it. I did not want to argue with a man who was about to take a knife to my flesh.

While he said good morning, and commented on the fine early autumn weather, and asked how I was feeling, he washed his hands, and pulled on a pair of surgical gloves, and checked the instruments the nurse was laying out. He told me again that it was a simple procedure. He repeated that there was no reason on earth for me to be walking around with an eyesore like that. He said he had performed the procedure dozens of times. He sat on the small black leather stool and used his feet to scuttle toward me.

"I've removed the other kind too. Fascinating case a few years ago." He looked up from my number to the space above my head. "A tattoo on the inside of the upper arm." He raised his right hand to the inside of his left arm to indicate the place. "About that long." He held up his hand with his thumb and forefinger an inch apart. "SS would be my guess."

I had forgotten that was on the left too. SS or prisoner, we carried the sign on the same side. My boyhood Latin came back to me. We carried it on the sinister side.

The doctor was rubbing a piece of cotton on my arm now, not on the number, but above it. The sensation was bracing, like aftershave.

"As I understand it, they were functional." He took the syringe from the nurse with his left hand. So he was sinister too. "They used them to indicate blood type. In case they were wounded and needed a transfusion." He bent over my arm. "I removed it entirely." I felt the needle pierce my flesh. "Not a trace. No scar. Nothing." I watched the liquid sink in the syringe. "You could see that man at the beach today, Mr. van Pels, and you wouldn't have an inkling what he had been up to." He withdrew the needle. "Like I always say, that's modern plastic surgery for you. We erase the past." I felt a peculiar sensation spreading.

Without taking his eyes from my arm, he held his left hand

out to the nurse again. "Of course, I'm just guessing." She slapped an instrument into it. "He didn't say it was an SS tattoo, and I sure didn't ask." He smirked down at my number. The Nazi who passed was our little joke.

I tried to pull my arm back.

His grip tightened. "There's nothing to be afraid of," he said without looking up. "You won't feel a thing."

I tugged again.

"You'll have to stay still, Mr. van Pels."

I wrenched my arm out of his grip. "I've changed my mind."

"It's a minor procedure. As I said, you won't feel a thing."

"I've changed my mind." I had not meant to shout. "I don't want it removed. You have no right to remove it."

He put down the scalpel and stood. His eyes focused on my face for a moment, just long enough for the disgust to register on his own. "Up to you." He turned and started out of the room. The nurse fluttered after him. His words seeped back to me just before the door closed.

"Very unstable, these people."

I INSISTED on driving home. Madeleine did not argue. She had no idea my left arm was numb. She did not even remark on the fact that I was driving with one hand. These days she was accustomed to it. But she could not help asking, as I gunned the engine to pass a car that was dawdling in the fast lane, and sped by billboards for gasoline and toothpaste and used car dealers, what had made me change my mind.

"It just seemed like a bad idea."

"It didn't last night. Or for the past two weeks. Isn't that when you first saw the doctor?"

So we were back to that. "I didn't want to worry you. That's why I didn't tell you about seeing him."

She did not answer.

"Are you saying you're disappointed?"

"That you didn't tell me?"

"That I'm not having the number removed?"

"I didn't want you to have it removed in the first place."

I glanced over at her. She was sitting at the far end of the front seat with her back against the passenger door. I did not let the children sit that way. It was dangerous. "Don't lean against the door." She shifted position. "If you didn't want me to do it, why didn't you say so?"

"When? At eleven o'clock last night? On the way in this morning?"

"You should have told me."

"You should—" she started, then stopped.

"Why didn't you want me to do it?"

"I didn't not want you to do it."

"Make up your mind. You didn't want me to do it, but you didn't not want me to do it."

"I wanted you to do it, if you wanted to. But I didn't think it was necessary."

"Necessary?"

"There's nothing wrong with it."

"The woman who will not even pierce her ears is telling me there's nothing wrong with walking around with a number tattooed on my arm."

"What I mean is I'm accustomed to it."

"*You*'re accustomed to it. Then that makes it all right. Then it's goddamn wonderful to walk around with a number tattooed on my arm."

"I didn't say that either. All I said was that it's part of you." She hesitated. Another wall of billboards raced by. Spark plugs and breakfast cereal and automobile tires. "Without it, you wouldn't be you."

What a stupid thing to say, I wanted to shout. "Stop leaning against the door," I told her.

I WAITED until Madeleine fell asleep. She knew about the safe in the back of the linen closet. She had watched me install it with my own hands shortly after we moved into the house. I had never given her the combination, not because I did not trust her, merely because I kept forgetting to write it down for her. But nothing in the safe was a secret from her. Everything in it was for her, her and the children.

I listened to her breathing grow deep and regular, then measured another five minutes by the clock on the night table. When I was sure I would not wake her, I got out of bed, padded across the room, giving the silent butler next to the closet and the chair in the corner a wide berth, and closed the door behind me. I did not want the light to disturb her. I shut the door to the girls' rooms too. Though the contents of the safe was for them, they were too young to know about such things.

I switched on the hall light and opened the door to the linen closet. Cleanliness filled my lungs. I took out the stacks of towels on the shelf in front of the safe with care, not because I was worried Madeleine would notice I had been at the safe again, merely because I did not want to undo her, or Mrs. Goralski's, tidiness. I am not an inconsiderate man.

I pulled open the false door cut in the back of the closet. The steel safe glinted in the light from the overhead fixture. I reached in and began to turn the knob. Eight to the right, four to the left, six to the right. The month and year I arrived in America. My fingertips felt the numbers click into place. Just opening the lock gave me pleasure.

I swung the door wide. The sight of the official-looking passport and fat manila envelope always went through me like a shot of whiskey, half adrenaline, half relaxation. I slid out the passport. The imitation leather cover was smooth between my fingers. The gold stamp and lettering—United States of America—winked up at me. I opened it reverently as a prayer book. Black letters marched across the thick paper. *Van Pels, Peter*; *wife, Madeleine*; *daughter, Abigail*; *daughter, Elizabeth*. As soon as the baby was born, I would add another name.

I slid it back into the safe and lifted out the manila envelope. It was heavier than the small blue document. I unwound the string around the clasp and lifted the flap. The money lay sleeping inside, sorted into piles, each held by two rubber bands. I took them out, arranged them neatly on the shelf, then put down the envelope so I would have both hands free to count. The doctor was wrong. You could not undo the past. That was why I had walked out of his office. I was embarrassed by the incident at first, but no longer. I had done the right thing. It was not that without the number I would not be me. Madeleine was wrong about that. It was merely that trying to undo the past was just another way of living in the past. I was interested in the future.

That was why I kept the passport up to date and added money to the envelope on a regular basis. My life was better than my wildest dreams back in the DP camp had envisioned. But I like to be prepared for all eventualities.

I slid the envelope back into the safe, spun the lock, and returned to the bedroom as quietly as I had left it.

I was just dozing off when I felt Madeleine press herself against my back. Her arm insinuated itself beneath mine, her hand came to rest on my chest, the baby pressed against the small of my back.

"Is everything still there?"

"What do you mean?"

"The safe. Isn't that what you were doing?"

"I just wanted to check something."

She nuzzled my ear. "It was a joke, not a complaint."

"I tried not to wake you."

"*You* didn't wake me. Your absence did."

I reached back and hooked my leg around one of hers. She moved her hand from my chest to my arm. Her fingertips grazed the number. At first I thought it was an accident, then I realized she knew what she was touching. She had zeroed in on it.

"To what extent do we remain obligated to the world even when we have been expelled from it?"
—*Men In Dark Times,*
by Hannah Arendt

TEN

■　■ I DID NOT HEAR THE CRY that announced my son's
■　■ arrival. The waiting area was some distance from the delivery room, where they had wheeled Madeleine less than an hour earlier. He arrived that quickly. My son, like me, was impatient.

I had thought I was a lucky man before. Now I could not believe my good fortune. The moment I saw him, before that, the minute the doctor told me it was a boy, every reservation I had about having a son fell away. The problem was not insurmountable. What was I saying? There was no problem. I had a choice in the matter, and I had already made it. I would not let anything interfere with this joy.

Just as I had been numbered as my father was, the same number, off by only one digit, so I had been cut as my father was, the same cut of Abraham, the same sign of the covenant. I did not believe in the covenant. I was no longer a Jew. There was no reason to circumcise my son. On the other hand, there was no reason not to. In America, many gentiles were circumcised, including George Johnson, who belonged to the country club that would not let my wife cross the threshold. I knew, because before George found out about Madeleine, he had invited me to play golf there, and I had taken a careful look around the locker room. I was in good company. At least, I was not alone. That steamy basement, simmering with musky deodorant and mellow whiskey and good-natured razzing, was a long way from a cattle car full of Polish resistance fighters, but sound carries. Drop your pants, drop your pants. There were hundreds of stories like that. Blond youths masquerading as Aryans, three-year-old boys hiding with Catholic nuns, Italians and French and Greeks and Dutch, all passing as nationals, inferior to the master race certainly, but not Jews, until the cry came to drop their pants. When they shouted that at my son, what would he say? That in America not only Jews were circumcised? That even George Johnson, who was as anti-Semitic as they, if more discreet about it, was cut as he was? I did not think the answer would carry much weight. I was not willing to take the chance.

I had made up my mind. I would not circumcise David. Madeleine had originally suggested that if the baby was a boy, we name him after my father. Then she remembered whom she was dealing with. Jews named children after dead relatives, gentiles after themselves.

"Unless, of course, you want to call him Peter. It will drive my parents crazy." To my in-laws, naming a baby after a living individual would be tempting fate to strike the individual dead on the spot, but Madeleine was not superstitious, and by now I knew the prospect of driving her parents crazy did not entirely displease her.

I said I had no desire to name a son after me. No man should have to carry the weight of his father. As for my own father, I told Madeleine it would be cruel to send a Hermann, even a Herman, out into an Indian Hills crowded with Marks and Scotts and Barrys. We decided on David. I liked the sound. And the name was ecumenical. There was David in the Old Testament, of course, but there was also David the patron saint of Wales. The Old Testament David took on Goliath. Saint David was usually portrayed with a dove on his shoulder. I was covering all my bets.

THE FIRST time I saw him was through a glass window. He was crying. His arms churned the air of the nursery, and his legs squirmed inside the tightly wrapped blanket, and his mouth was a tiny black hole in his furious red face. I stood waiting for a nurse to pick him up. No one seemed to hear him. I could not understand it. I was on the other side of the glass, and I heard his screams. It was unconscionable. It was sadistic. I formed my hand into a fist and rapped my knuckles against the window. A nurse with bleached yellow hair sticking untidily out of her cap looked up. A light knock on the window caught her attention, but a howling baby did not. I pointed to my son. She stood staring at me. Please, I mouthed. As my father-in-law is fond of saying, you get more flies with honey than vinegar. She shook her head in disapproval, but took the few steps to the bassinet and picked up David. It took a minute or so of patting and bouncing until the howls subsided. I pantomimed a thank-you and bowed. She shook her head again, but this time she smiled. It would serve her right if I reported her, but I would not report her. I would not ruin this momentous day with petty complaints. And the last thing I wanted was to upset my wife. I would have fallen to my knees and thanked her for the gift of our son, if I were that kind of man, which I am not. But I had bought her something to show her how grateful I was. A diamond pin is nothing to sneeze at. It was more expensive than the gold bracelet I had given her when Abigail was born and the pearls for Betsy, not because David's birth was more significant, but because I was making more money.

I started down the hall to Madeleine's room. The small jeweler's box in my pocket rubbed against my leg with each step. I hoped she would like the pin. I was sorry I had not bought the earrings after all. The jeweler said buying diamond earrings for a woman who had not pierced her ears was foolhardy, but foolhardy was how I felt. I had a son. There was nothing I would not do for him and his sisters. There was nothing I would not give their mother. All she had to do was ask.

Madeleine was sitting up in the hospital bed, her short curls plastered to her head, an unhealthy green tinge to her skin, though that might have been the reflection of the hospital walls. She did not look her best, and I loved her more than ever. Of course, I did not say that. She did not have to be told how she looked a few hours after giving birth. And she knew I loved her.

I crossed the room to the bed. As she pushed herself up with the palms of her hands, her mouth shriveled into a grimace. I really did love her more than ever. She shifted to make room for me on the side of the bed. I sat and took her hand. The skin felt dry as tissue paper. I leaned in to kiss her. She smelled medicinal and milky.

She asked if I had seen David and wasn't he the best-looking baby in the nursery, and I said I had and he was, and did not mention that I had had to bang on the window to get a nurse to pick him up. I did not want to worry her. And she did not like it when I made demands she thought unreasonable, though I cannot see anything unreasonable in asking a nurse to comfort a screaming baby. It's her job, for Christ's sake.

"The pediatrician came by," she said as she leaned back against the pillows. "He wanted to know about the circumcision. I told him no religious ceremony. We want a simple medical procedure performed by him, or one of his minions."

"One of his minions?"

"Sometimes a resident does it. That's okay with me. As long as it's a properly trained doctor. I am not about to let someone who doesn't know the first thing about modern medicine take a knife to our son. No matter what my parents say."

"We'll discuss it."

"That means Daddy's been after you again. There's nothing to discuss. He's our son, and you and I agreed. No religious ceremony."

We had agreed on nothing, but I would not argue with her now. She was too weak. She was too excitable.

"I meant we'll discuss whether we're going to do anything at all."

"What do you mean? He has to be circumcised."

"Why?"

"Because that's what they do to little boys these days. It's accepted medical practice."

"So were leeches at one time."

"Be serious, Peter. All the books say it's healthier."

"Ah, the books." What did the books know? Where were the books when the men came through the train shouting drop your pants, drop your pants?

"The pediatrician says so too."

"The pediatrician's name is Caneglio."

"What does that have to do with anything?"

"Mrs. Caneglio goes to mass every Sunday."

"I'm still not following you," she said, though from the way her long eyes narrowed, I had a feeling she was.

"Dr. Caneglio does not have to worry about his son's being mistaken for a Jew."

Her head jerked back, as if I had slapped her. "Mistaken?"

"You know what I mean."

"If you didn't want your son mistaken for a Jew, you shouldn't have married me."

"I thought we agreed. Neither of us believes in anything."

"I'm not talking about believing in anything. I'm talking about being Jewish. That's what I am. Which means David is half Jewish. According to Jewish law, which I don't care about, but according to it, he's completely Jewish. If the mother is, the child is. So it's a little late to start worrying about having your son mistaken for a Jew."

Why didn't I tell her the truth then? She would have been

relieved, not that I was a Jew, but that I was not some of the other things she was beginning to fear. She would have been thrilled. I was not just any Jew. I was Anne Frank's Jew. But to tell her that would have been to return to that. I could not do it.

"You have not seen the things I have," was all I said.

She looked as if I had slapped her again, but this time she did not answer. She could not argue with my past.

"We'll discuss it," I repeated, though I had made up my mind we would not. If I did not protect my son, who would?

I took the velvet box from my pocket and held it out to her. She made no move to take it. "Open it," I said. She sat staring at it. She was too exhausted even to open the box. I flipped up the top for her. The diamond pin winked from the black satin lining. She was so overwhelmed, she began to cry.

THE HOUSE was dark. I had never realized how sinister it looked in the night. I missed the amber holes the lighted windows punched into the blackness. I missed knowing my wife and children were inside.

As I turned into the driveway, my headlights raked the shrubbery. Something, a neighbor's cat, a raccoon, darted through the beam and disappeared into the darkness.

I eased the car next to Madeleine's station wagon, climbed out, and let myself in through the back door. The silence was as thick as the darkness. Susannah had taken the girls to spend the night with her. I was sorry now I had agreed to the arrangement. The sooner I had Madeleine and the girls and David under my roof, the happier I would be.

I went through the house turning on lights. Then I hung up my coat in the front closet, got out of my jacket and tie, and took a glass from the cabinet and an ice tray from the freezer. I am not a drinking man. I will have a whiskey with business associates, when it is called for. I have been known to get a little happy at weddings and other family celebrations. I am not averse to a cocktail when we go out to dinner on some occasion. But I am not the sort of man who walks into the house in the evening and heads straight for the liquor cabinet. Tonight, however, I had cause for celebration. I had a son, an uncircumcised son who would never be mistaken for a Jew, no matter what Madeleine said. I had made the right decision.

I went to the sideboard in the dining room, picked up the bottle of Chivas Regal my father-in-law always brings when he comes to visit, though he is no more a drinking man than I am, and filled the glass halfway. As I carried it back to the kitchen, I caught sight of my reflection in the long windows at the end of the eating area. They were slippery with darkness. I lifted my glass in a toast to my son. The figure in the window lifted his in return. We drank.

I put the glass down on the counter and took the cast-iron casserole with the pot roast and the Corning Ware dishes filled with string beans and potatoes out of the refrigerator. Just as Madeleine had kept an overnight bag packed for several weeks now, she had made sure that the refrigerator was stocked with leftovers to tide me over while she was gone. My hunger had moderated, but its reputation lingered.

Instructions were Scotch-taped to the various pots and dishes to tell me how to heat them up. I followed the directions, then went back to the dining room and refilled my glass while I waited for everything to warm. When the food was ready, I heaped it onto a plate and carried it to one end of the kitchen table. I rarely ate dinner alone at this table. I had eaten by myself for a few nights after each of my daughters was born. There was another time, too. It took me a moment to place it. I had come downstairs in the middle of the night, taken out half the refrigerator, and carried it to the table. Madeleine had followed me a little while later. I could see her expression as she opened the louvered doors to the kitchen. She blinked against the bright light. She put a hand up to her sleep-rumpled face to shut out the glare. Her eyes narrowed as the absurd banquet came into focus. Her gaze crawled over the table. It came to a stop when it reached the jar of baby food. I said something about thinking it was regular applesauce and carried it back to the refrigerator, but it was too late. I knew what she was thinking. What kind of man takes food out of the mouths of children? She could not imagine. The refrigerators of her childhood had been stuffed with ripe fruit and cream-capped milk and leftovers spoiling to be thrown away. In the annex, we could have lived for a week on the leftovers thrown out of my mother-in-law's refrigerator in one day. To my wife, hunger was a missed lunch, starvation the name of a diet to lose weight. The sight of me racked by it that night had scandalized her. Her eyes had narrowed, and her mouth had curled in disgust, and she had looked at me as if I were a stranger. She had looked at me just as she had in the hospital room earlier this evening, when I told her I would not circumcise our son, because I could not take the chance of his being mistaken for a Jew.

I stood and picked up my plate. I had not thought I was hungry, but suddenly I wanted more. I felt as if I could devour the entire hunk of meat, a week's worth of sustenance. As I turned, I caught a glimpse of myself in the long windows at the end of the breakfast room again. Moments earlier a young man, a new father, had toasted me in those windows. Now an old man, his shoulders rounded, his face carved with want, peered back at me from under heavy eyelids. When had I begun to resemble my father?

I straightened my shoulders and lifted my chin, but I could still see my father's hooded eyes in the black glass. The stubborn line of mouth was his too. I took another swallow of my drink. The man who resembled my father swallowed too. Congratulations, I said and bowed. He bowed in return. A fine thing, I told him, and he agreed. A son. To carry on the name, the one I had not changed, I reassured him. The one I had not had to, he reminded me.

David van Pels, I insisted.

David van Pels, the figure in the glass repeated. We each raised a hand and wiped an eye with the back of it.

Except for one thing.

I knew what was coming. But I had not given in to my wife, and I was not going to capitulate to this figment of my imagination. I knew he was no more than that. I was not one of the damaged, those scarred souls who cross streets when they see policemen, and stand paralyzed with terror as a siren grows louder, and hallucinate the presence of the dead. The term for the condition, German of course, is Verfolgungsbedingt. It means the trouble, whatever it is, is the result of what the individual endured at the hands of the Nazis. It also means the poor wretch is entitled to a pittance of financial compensation

from the German government. That is why Verfolgungsbedingt
is so hard to prove. I have read about some of the rulings by
German psychiatric boards. Plagued by depression? What does
that have to do with the fact that each week for months on end,
you stood in a line of fifteen-year-old girls, counting off numbers, eight, nine, ten, eleven, not knowing whether on that particular day the odds or the evens were marked for death? Suffer
hallucinations? Surely, that is not related to your being made to
witness the shooting of your father, mother, older brother, and
three sisters.

I cannot do it, I said. It's too dangerous.

I thought you were in America now. The land of opportunity. The home of the free and the brave. The country of circumcised penises.

I am. I'm an American citizen. We all are. The whole family.

So tell me, what's the good of that, if you live as if you're
back in that stinking annex? Tell me, my big successful son
with a nice house, and a thriving business, and a safe full of
cash for the getaway.

I didn't have the number removed. I kept that for you.

You think that's it? You keep the number, and you can wash
your hands of me? Of your mother and me, both?

I'm not washing my hands of you. I'm just trying to protect
my son. That's what a father does for his children.

What are you saying? That I didn't protect you? I got you to
Amsterdam, didn't I? The Netherlands stayed neutral in the
last war. How was I to know it wouldn't this time?

Other people knew.

I put us on the emigration list. Even before the war started.

Still not soon enough.

So what are you telling me, I waited too long?

You did, goddammit.

Don't you speak that way to me. I'm still your father. The Nazis couldn't undo that, and neither can you.

I'm not trying to. Just because I don't run around broadcasting that I'm a Jew, doesn't mean I've betrayed you.

Broadcasting? You call telling your wife and children broadcasting? But I don't care about that. I care about my grandson. He should be like me, and you, and my father. That's all I'm asking. A little respect. A line of connection. It's the least you can do for me.

You're dead, for God's sake.

My father went on staring from the window. That's why you have to do this for me.

A CLEAN-CUT young man in a starched white jacket cut my son's foreskin without any attendant ritual, and though David let out a shriek of protest, there were no other immediate consequences, except perhaps the inordinate, if surreptitious, attention I could not help paying to other infants as they were being diapered and grown men standing at urinals. The count was reassuring. If they came through the train in America these days, half the population would be chosen.

THE NIGHT before Madeleine and the baby were to come home from the hospital, I deposited another six hundred dollars in the manila envelope in the safe in the linen closet. I had already taken care of adding David's name to the passport. The money had nothing to do with the fact that I had allowed them to circumcise my son. I put in more money every few months. We were five now. The cost of living was going up, though the longer I kept putting money in, the more certain I was I would never have to take it out.

"He [Pfeffer] was a handsome man, a charmer who resembled the romantic French singer Maurice Chevalier.... He was a very appealing person."

—Anne Frank Remembered: The Story of
the Woman Who Helped to Hide the Frank Family,
by Miep Gies with Alison Leslie Gold

"There was still the problem of the sagging second act [of The Diary of Anne Frank].... On September 8, after the rehearsal ... [the playwrights, director, and producer] found the solution: Mr. van Daan would steal some bread."

—The Real Nick and Nora: Frances Goodrich
and Albert Hackett, Writers of Stage and
Screen Classics, by David L. Goodrich

ELEVEN

WHEN I GOT HOME THAT EVENING, Madeleine was wearing a black wool suit, high heels that stretched the calves of her legs like harp strings, and pearls, not the long double strand I bought her when Betsy was born, which she saves for evenings, but the girlish single strand her parents gave her when she turned sixteen. She had been somewhere, but I could not for the life of me remember where, though she must have told me.

"It was wonderful," she said.

I had not yet taken off my coat.

"What was wonderful?"

"The play."

Now I remembered. I could not imagine how it had slipped my mind. She and Susannah had taken the train to New York to see a matinee performance of *The Diary of Anne Frank*. There was nothing unusual about that. My wife and her sister often go to matinees without their husbands. Neither Norman nor I enjoy fighting the traffic to get into the city, and rushing through dinner to make the curtain, and sitting in an over-heated theater with knees under our chins—Norman is almost as tall as I am—and coats bunched on our laps, and someone breathing garlic from a French dinner down our necks for two and a half hours. Susannah had tried to get Norman to make an exception for this play, but Norman insisted that no sane man would want to spend a Saturday night watching eight actors pretending to be locked in a couple of airless rooms, waiting for death. I backed up Norman. Neither of us liked Tennessee Williams, another of our wives' favorites, either. We could not stand all those unhappy people torturing one another, in unintelligible accents, for no good reason.

Unlike her sister, Madeleine had not tried to convince me to see *The Diary of Anne Frank*. She knew no particulars about my life during the war, only that I had somehow survived in Amsterdam, a hardship but not an impossibility for a gentile, then ended up in Auschwitz for refusing to sign the pledge of loyalty to the German Reich required of all Dutch students. I never told her that was the reason, though I had mentioned the pledge, but somehow, as she grew more indignant over the McCarthy hearings, she came to believe it. My courage thrilled her, my foolhardiness worried her, and the thought of them both convinced her that a play about Amsterdam under the occupation would cut too close for comfort. She was wrong. I admit the book upset me, when I first saw it, but that had been years ago. The play was at one more remove. I would barely recognize the characters. I could harbor only antipathy for a bunch of actors impersonating them. A few years later, when a play about Franklin Roosevelt called *Sunrise at Campobello* ran on Broadway, a reporter asked Eleanor Roosevelt what she thought of it. Mrs. Roosevelt said it was an entertaining show, but it had nothing to do with anyone she knew. That was the way I felt about *The Diary of Anne Frank,* without even seeing it.

"It was marvelous," Madeleine said now. Marvelous is not a word my wife customarily uses, and I could tell from that, and the clipped staccato of her speech, and the straight-backed way she sat at the kitchen table while the girls ate dinner, that part of her was still back in the Cort Theater watching Joseph Schildkraut as Otto Frank and Gusti Huber as Mrs. Frank and Susan Strasberg as Anne. The part of Peter was played by an actor called David Levin. I did not want to see the play, but somehow I had gleaned a considerable amount of information about it. I had even walked past the theater once when I was in the city. I forget what had taken me there that night. The black letters marched across the neon marquis. As I stood staring up at them, a man came close. "Hey, buddy." My hands balled into fists before I even turned. He had a pig's snout for a nose. "Twenty bucks," he whispered. "Fifth row center. A steal." My fists unclenched. The man was not a thug, only a scalper. I told him I was not interested, but as I turned away and started down Forty-eighth Street, I could not help laughing at the insanity. Twenty dollars for a four-eighty ticket. Anne would have been proud.

I carried my coat to the hall closet. Madeleine stood and followed me.

"It was heart-wrenching." Another expression she does not toss around every day of the week.

"I bet," I said and went back to the kitchen. She followed me.

"But there were funny parts too."

So it was a comedy.

I took a glass from the cabinet, opened the freezer, and slid out an ice tray. As I said, I am not a drinking man, but I felt the need for a drink that night. The local painters' union was threatening to strike over the issue of spray painting, again.

I dropped two cubes in my glass, carried it to the sideboard in the dining room, half filled it with scotch, and carried it back to the kitchen. My wife dogged my steps.

"It's the best thing I've seen in years."

I sat at the table between my daughters and placed the glass in front of me. "I'm glad you enjoyed it."

"I'm not sure enjoy is the right word, but it did make me understand certain things."

By certain things she meant me. I was not going to tell her that sitting in a theater for two and a half hours watching actors pretend to be hungry and frightened and doomed was not going to help her understand me. I was not even going to explain that I did not want her to understand me. I loved her for not understanding me. That was the reason I had kept walking when the girl at the Marseilles had given me smiles thin as new dimes. I had not thought of that girl in years. I would not think of her again once Madeleine stopped carrying on about the play.

"So," I said to Abigail, "what's the news from Mrs. Gleckler's class?"

She held one arm out for me to examine. The fragility of it still frightened me. There was a Band-Aid on her elbow.

"If you'd rather not hear about this," Madeleine said.

"I'm listening," I told her. "What happened?" I asked Abigail.

"Laurie pushed me."

"I cried at the end," Madeleine said. "The whole audience was in tears."

"Did you push Laurie back?" I asked Abigail.

Abby grinned and nodded.

"Good girl!"

"She was in hiding for two years," Madeleine said, "and she died in a concentration camp." She dropped her voice on the last two words, as if they were not fit for childish ears, as if our daughters would understand them any more than she did. "But she never lost her faith in mankind."

I swiveled to Betsy. Her face and hands were covered with food, but her plate was still full. My daughters' refusal to eat always filled me with confusion. Did they not know what hunger was? Thank god they did not know what hunger was. "Boy, those carrots look good." I smacked my lips.

"Tell me if you don't want to hear about it," Madeleine said again.

I should not have had to tell her. "I'm listening," I repeated and picked up the spoon from Betsy's plate.

"The most amazing part, the thing that saves it from being unbearable, is the triumph of the human spirit."

Now we were into the human spirit.

"The father, Otto Frank, is still alive. That's how the play starts. With his finding the diary."

I took a swallow of my drink.

"I can't imagine," Madeleine said, "what that must be like."

She was right. She could not. So why in hell did she insist on talking about it? I lifted the spoon to Betsy's mouth. Betsy pressed her lips together.

"You know what else was fascinating? The way the different characters responded to the situation. There were two families in hiding, and a single man. The man, Dussel was his name, was a complete fool."

"That's what dussel means." I had not meant to speak. I would not stop her from talking about it, but I did not want to encourage the discussion.

"I didn't know that."

"You don't speak German."

"What a coincidence. That he's a fool and has the name of one."

"For Christ's sake, Madeleine. She made up the name." I nudged the spoon against my daughter's closed mouth. Betsy shook her head back and forth. "At least, that's my guess."

"Of course. I should have known that. Anyway, this Dussel character really is a buffoon, but the third man, the other father, Mr. van Daan, is worse."

"Worse how?" I could have bitten my tongue.

"He was a thief."

I pried the spoon between my daughter's lips. Her mouth opened to let out her rage, the opportunity I was waiting for. I shoved the spoon in.

"It's the most awful scene. One night Mrs. Frank hears a

noise and gets up, and there's Mr. van Daan, the father of the boy Ann's in love with, stealing bread from the cupboard. All the time they thought it was the rats, it was really him. He. Taking food out of his own child's mouth. Can you imagine?"

"That never happened," I said above my daughter's wails.

"What?"

I shoveled in another spoonful of food. "I mean, no, I can't imagine that could happen. Maybe it didn't. It's only a play."

"Based on the diary, though."

My daughter shrieked. I stoked.

"The diary was real," Madeleine insisted. "So the father must have done it."

The spoon clattered to the floor. I had not thrown it. It had slipped.

"Goddammit, Madeleine, you're the college graduate. Haven't you ever heard of dramatic license?" I pushed myself away from the table and stood. "And while you're worrying about who's eating what, why don't you pay some attention to your own daughter? Why don't you try to get a decent meal down her instead of worrying about a bunch of fat happy actors who don't even know what hunger is?"

It would have been bad enough if I had stopped there. Perhaps if I had bothered to look at the upturned faces, my daughters' stained with food, all three with surprise and fear, I would have. But I was not looking at my wife and daughters. I was staring beyond their thin shoulders, over their gleaming heads, to another group gathered around another table, faces hollow-cheeked, hair dull from dirt and malnutrition, stomachs aching with hunger. I blinked my eyes against those other diners, but they would not go away.

"Like you. Like this whole damn family. Picking at plates, throwing perfectly good food down the garbage disposal. It makes me sick to my stomach," I shouted as I lurched out of the kitchen.

I went down to the family room and switched on the television. Grinning gray faces leered back at me. Mouths opened and closed. Voices brayed. I got up and turned down the volume. Now I could hear them in the kitchen.

Madeleine carried the tune while my daughters' sobs kept the beat. "Daddy didn't mean it. Mommy said some silly things, that's all. Mommy should have known better. Daddy's not angry at you."

I stood and turned up the volume on the television again.

When I looked up a few minutes later, my daughters were standing at the top of the stairs. Their eyes were hard little marbles of distrust, their mouths slits of suspicion.

"Come on," I said, "come keep me company."

Betsy, the adventuress, took a single hesitant step down. Abigail, no fool, stayed where she was.

I spread my arms wide along the back of the sofa in twin invitations. "Come on," I repeated. Betsy took another step. Abigail did not move.

"Pretty please," I begged.

Betsy took one more step.

"With whipped cream on top."

She came down the last two stairs and hurled herself across the room and onto the sofa. Abigail waited until her sister had settled in the crook of my arm. She was wary, my firstborn. When she was convinced it was not a trick, that I would not turn into a monster again, she followed her sister across the room and sat on my other side. I circled their shoulders and pulled them close. "It's all right," I sang over the sound of the television. "Everything is going to be all right." They were a father's words, though my own father had never lied them to me.

WHEN I climbed the stairs to the kitchen half an hour later, Madeleine was standing at the sink with her back to the door. She had taken off the jacket of her suit and slipped an apron over her skirt and blouse. One high-heeled pump lay on its side. Her weight rested on her stockinged foot, throwing one hip higher than the other. The stance was roguish, but I knew that was not her intent.

"Do you want me to get your slippers?"

She shook her head no. The curls of her poodle cut brushed the back of her collar.

"I'm sorry."

She did not answer.

"I can't imagine what got into me."

She shut off the water, picked up a towel, and turned to me. A line of mascara ran down one cheek. "If you wanted me to stop talking about it, you should have said so. I asked if you minded. I said do you want me to stop."

"It's not that."

"Then what? I don't understand."

That's the point. You don't. You can't. I don't want you to. "Let's just forget it."

She stood staring at me across the appliance-humming kitchen.

"You have mascara on your cheek."

She reached up and rubbed her left cheek.

"The right one."

She rubbed her other cheek. The black line became a smudge. I could have crossed the kitchen and wiped it off. I stood where I was. She turned back to the sink.

"Just do me one favor," she said.

"Anything." I meant it.

"Don't bring me flowers tomorrow. Don't bring me flowers, and don't bring the girls anything either."

"What do you mean?"

"I mean that's what you always do after something like this."

"Something like this? You make it sound as if it's a regular occurrence."

She did not answer. She did not even turn around, but I knew from the rhythmic movement of her shoulders, almost like the motion of those men praying in the synagogue I had gone to after I regained my voice, that she was crying again. It was not fair. This was not a regular occurrence. We never fought.

THE NEXT night I stopped on the way home from the office and bought a camellia plant. She had said not to buy her flowers, but I knew she did not mean it. Besides, this was not a bouquet that would die in a few days, but a plant that would continue to bloom.

"Gusti [Huber] was the first actress in Austria to be cleared
by the American military government."
—Joseph Besch, formerly Captain Besch,
U.S. Army, husband of Gusti Huber,
quoted in the newspaper column "Broadway Discovers"

"Gusti Huber . . . portrays Mrs. Frank. . . . A top stage and
screen star in war time nazi Germany, she appeared in
numerous motion pictures. . . . In 1943, while the real Mrs.
Frank remained in constant fear for the lives of her dear
ones, Gusti Huber charmed the Germans in a movie entitled
'Gabrielle Dambrone.' . . . In 1944, when the Frank family
was shipped off in sealed cars, Miss Huber amused the citizens of the Third Reich with her starring performance. . . .
At the very same time Anne was murdered in Bergen-
Belsen, Gusti was busy shooting a screen comedy. . . . I am
wondering if she would have uttered the word 'Sholom'
from the stage—had Hitler won the war."
—Herbert G. Luft, *American Jewish Ledger*,
Newark, New Jersey, March 28, 1956

TWELVE

■ ■ MADELEINE WAS SITTING AT the table when I came into
■ ■ the kitchen that evening, her tortoiseshell glasses on her
nose, the old portable typewriter she had used in college in
front of her. She often took the typewriter out of the back of
the hall closet in behalf of the League of Women Voters, and

the Women's League for Peace and Freedom, and a variety of other good causes. In the months before the Rosenbergs were executed, she had rarely put it away. These days it came out less often, but it was out tonight.

I said I was sorry I was late, and, still typing, she told me David was asleep, but she had just put the girls to bed, and I had time to say good night to them. Her fingers flew over the keys. She was an excellent typist, thanks to my father-in-law, who had insisted both his daughters have a marketable skill, in case fortune dealt them an unexpected blow and someday they had to earn their own living. I envied his definition of an unexpected blow.

I went upstairs to say goodnight to my daughters. Madeleine must have been so engrossed in whatever she was doing that she had lost track of time. They were already asleep. I stood in the doorway studying them in the dim glow that rose like a pink and blue mist from the butterfly-shaped nightlight plugged into a socket in the corner. Abigail slept neat and compact as a mummy, her arms at her side, her face a scrubbed moon drifting over the landscape of her flowered quilt. Betsy sprawled across her bed as if she had been dropped from a great height. Face down, arms and legs at sharp angles to her small body, she reminded me of something. It took me a moment to figure out what. She looked like a human swastika. I stepped into the room, bent to her bed, and straightened her arms and legs. Then I pulled the covers over her and went back downstairs.

Madeleine was still at the table. Her hands continued to fly over the keys. She was in a hurry to finish. My wife did not like to be otherwise engaged when I arrived home in the evening.

McCall's, Ladies' Home Journal, and her mother warned that inattention was the first step on the downward path to wandering husbands and home-wrecking harpies hell-bent on becoming second wives. She did not believe the magazines or her mother, but she was not so secure in her convictions that she wanted to test the hypothesis.

I came up behind her, bent to kiss the top of her head, and reached under her moving arms to embrace her. She had stopped nursing, but her breasts were still swollen.

She shrugged her shoulders to shake me off. "I'll be through in a minute."

"What is it now? Starving children in Greece or Red-baiters in Washington?" I teased her about her causes, but I envied them, or at least her faith in them. How comforting to think that an irate letter could right wrongs, a densely signed petition save the world.

"Take a look at that." She nodded toward a newspaper spread open on the table. *Newark Star-Ledger* ran across the top of the page. We did not get the *Newark Star-Ledger.* Either someone had given it to her or told her to go out and buy it. This was a campaign.

I picked up the paper. The headline of the column on the left caught my attention.

GUSTI HUBER'S ROLE
IN ANNE FRANK DIARY

I was surprised. Madeleine had not mentioned the play since the night I had yelled at her and the girls about wasting food. The fact that she was bringing it up now was an indication of how incensed she must be. She did not want to upset me, but she could not turn a blind eye to injustice, whatever it might be in this instance.

"This document, in book and play form, has touched the hearts of hundreds of thousands of persons," I read.

I still could not understand why. Scores of people had gone into hiding. Millions had died. Nobody had cared. At least nobody had done anything to stop it. And no one wanted to hear about it now. Where you've been, what you've seen, it's not going to endear you to people. It had been true ten years ago. It was even more true today. Except for Anne. The world could not get enough of Anne. Susan Strasberg stared up from the glossy pages of half a dozen magazines, including the cover of *Life,* her complexion creamy, her eyes luminous, her hair lustrous. Anne should have looked so good in those days. We all should have. Members of the cast attested to the powerful emotions they experienced six nights a week and twice a day on Wednesdays and Saturdays. Teenage girls clipped pictures of the young man who played Peter and hung them on their walls, as Anne had hung pictures of movie stars and royalty above her bed. If Abigail were a few years older, a photograph of a boy who was playing the boy who was supposed to be the boy I once was would hang over her bed. I was ready for crushes on actors, but I could not permit this other enthusiasm, this thrall to misery and suffering. It had to stop.

Madeleine, I would say.

Yes? she would answer without lifting her eyes from the keys.

About this play.

Mmm.

I am Peter.

Would her head snap up from the typewriter? Would she tell me to stop joking, because this was not a laughing matter? Would she believe me? And if she did, then what? Would she take me to her bosom? Would she shoulder my suffering? Would she slip the silvery key of her love, brightly polished like all the other silver in the house, into the lock of my past and twist it? That I could not allow.

I looked down at the newspaper again and skimmed the rest of the column. It was about Gusti Huber, the actress who played the mother of Anne Frank on Broadway, but it was about her career before she came to America. It told how she had refused to work with Jewish actors and directors in Vienna before the war and continued making movies for the Nazis until the end of the war. "At the very same time Anne was murdered in Bergen-Belsen, Gusti was busy shooting a screen comedy entitled 'Wie ein Dieb in Der Nacht'—'As a Thief in the Night.'"

That was another thing I loved about America. Here this was still news.

"You wrote a letter to the editor?"

Madeleine stood, placed the typewriter back in its case, and snapped the locks shut. "A bit more than that." She picked up one of the letters and handed it to me.

Mr. Kermit Bloomgarden

1545 Broadway

New York 36, N.Y.

Bloomgarden was the producer of the play. That was another shard of information I had acquired without realizing it.

I skimmed the letter. My wife and hundreds of other women threatened to boycott the play if Gusti Huber was not replaced.

"You've already seen the play."

"He doesn't know that."

I glanced down at the table. It was strewn with papers. "Who else are you writing to?"

"The director. The playwrights. The Drama Guild. Actors' Equity."

I looked across the table at my wife. Her cheeks were crimson, her eyes a little wild. She looked the way she did after we made love. I glanced down at the table again. I could see no harm in a handful of letters to people who would probably not even read them. The producer and director were famous. The two playwrights had made their fortune writing movies about drunk husband-and-wife detectives with a small terrier, and Jimmy Stewart deciding not to commit suicide on Christmas Eve. I had no idea where I had picked up all this useless information. The play was making money. None of them would give a damn if the actress playing Mrs. Frank had performed for Hitler himself.

"And Otto Frank." The color on Madeleine's cheeks flamed. The heat of probity flickered in her eyes.

"What?"

"It's part of the campaign. There's a list of people to write to. Anne Frank's father is on it. I told you he's still alive. He lives in Switzerland."

"Switzerland," I repeated. I had seen his name on the Red Cross lists of survivors. I had read of him in articles about the published diary. But those reports had been as insubstantial as rumors. Now he was in my kitchen. I could no longer pretend not to believe in him. You're like a son to me, he used to say when I brought him food in the hospital at Auschwitz.

"Basel," Madeleine said. She picked up a letter from the table and read from it. "Herbstgasse 11, Basel, Switzerland."

I took the sheet of paper from her. "Dear Mr. Frank." My eye ran down the page. The letter was polite, even deferential. She felt sure that Mr. Frank did not know. She was certain he would not permit this sacrilege to his daughter's memory to continue. She assured him that his daughter's diary occupied a place in her heart and conscience. I reached the bottom of the page.

Sincerely,

Madeleine van Pels

(Mrs. Peter)

My mother-in-law, the Emily Post of north-central New Jersey, had trained her daughters well. For all my wife's strangled rebelliousness, she would no more sign a letter without the official Mrs. and my first name below her own than she would blow her nose in a dinner napkin or go to the theater without white gloves.

I could not permit it. When Otto had claimed me as his son, I had wanted a father. But I could not afford a father now, at least not one like Otto, who was in thrall to the past. If my own father had lived, it would have been different. I would never have turned my back on him. I swear it. You cannot judge a man by how he behaves on a station platform with dogs snapping at his legs and SS officers beating his head, or on a work detail in the crosshairs of a camp guard's rifle. But Otto was not my father. I admired him. I pitied him. But I would not accompany him on his maudlin journey into the past. I declined to crawl up those stairs into a world of darkness. I refused to risk myself and my family for his memories.

"You don't really intend to send this?"

"Why not?"

"Because it's cruel."

"He ought to be told. I'm sure he'd want to know. I would in his place."

There it was again, that reckless faith in the power of the vicarious.

"You think Otto Frank doesn't know? You think the man who wrote this article knows, and the people who are organizing this letter-writing campaign know, and now you and I know, but the father of the girl who wrote the diary does not know?"

"I can't believe he would permit it, if he did."

Perhaps she was right. Perhaps Otto did not know. Or perhaps he knew and still had not learned. When the man from the Green Police came to take us away and noticed the old footlocker from the First World War printed with Otto's name and rank in the German army, he practically snapped to attention, and a look of relief crossed Otto's face. This was more like it. This was the Germany he knew. Minutes later they pushed us down the stairs into the waiting van.

"Maybe it's not up to him. These things are arranged by contract. People buy and sell rights, just as they do property. If I sell a house, I cannot prevent the new owner from painting it an ugly color or adding unsightly additions. If this man, what did you say his name was, Otto Frank, if he sold the rights to the play, he probably has no say over who acts in it."

She stood looking at me. The color was draining from her cheeks. Her front teeth worried her lower lip. She is a soft-hearted woman, my wife.

"You think so?"

"I think that if he does not know, and he finds out and can do nothing about it, it will be torture. More torture. If others want to torment him, that's up to them. But I don't think you and I want to be part of it."

"I never thought of it that way."

"Now you do." I tore the letter I was holding in two. She flinched at the sound, but she did not protest.

My wife did not send any of the letters she had so furiously typed, though she did not know that. She gave them to me to mail the following morning. I took the neatly addressed envelopes from her hands and put them beside me on the front seat of the car. A few minutes later, as I sat waiting for the attendant to fill the gas tank, I tore the envelopes in two, just as I had ripped Otto's letter the night before. I threw half of them in the trash can in the gas station and tossed the other half in a big metal waste bin at the site. Mr. Bloomgarden and Mr. Kanin and the rest of them probably did not know that the people Anne called the van Daans were really the van Pels. But I did not want to take the chance.

THE PLAY ran for a year and a half. I got accustomed to seeing the ads, and hearing praise from people who were slower on the uptake than my wife and her sister, and, on the rare occasions when I let Madeleine drag me to another show, passing the photographs of actors in shabby clothes with suffering or frightened or laughing faces, staring out from the glassed-in panels in front of the Cort Theater. They had, as I said, nothing to do with me. Nonetheless, when I saw the article, only a paragraph really, in the paper, I could not resist. This was not for me. I was doing it for the children.

As I came through the door to the family room, my daughters looked away from the television, saw the carrying case in my hand, and were on their feet in a flash. They hurled themselves toward me. David followed, weaving on the balls of his feet like a small drunk. All three of them were hanging on me, and trying to peer into the case, and squealing and shrieking. Madeleine heard the noise and came down the stairs just in time to see the cat come strolling out of the case.

"What's that?" she asked.

"What does it look like?"

He did not hug the perimeters of the room as most cats would do on strange turf, but prowled straight across it. He was a fearless specimen, accustomed to bright lights and loud applause and strangers. He padded to the sofa, jumped up, strolled across the back, and leapt to the floor again. The children followed close on his tail.

"This is a surprise," Madeleine said.

"We've been talking about a pet."

"We have?"

"Sure, when the Wieners got their poodle."

"That was more than a year ago."

"If you don't want it . . ." I began, and my daughters shrieked in protest, as I knew they would.

Madeleine looked at me and shook her head. "You think I'm going to ask my children to choose between me and a small furry animal? No, I like the idea, but how come you didn't get a kitten?"

"This one needed a home."

"Why?"

There was no reason not to tell her the truth. According to the paragraph in the paper, when *The Diary of Anne Frank* closed, neither the actors nor the stagehands nor anyone else connected with the production wanted to take the cat who had played Mouschi. There was nothing Madeleine would like better than having a cat with that pedigree. I could hear her telling the story now. And you'll never guess where it came from.

"One of the workmen brought it to the site," I said. "It turns out his wife is allergic."

"Is it a girl or a boy?" Abigail asked.

"A tom. That means a boy."

Betsy was trying to wrangle the cat into her lap. "Can we name him?"

"You can try, but he already has a name. He answers to Mouschi."

At the sound, the cat streaked away from Betsy and bounded into my lap.

"There's a destructive urge in people, the urge to rage, murder, and kill."

—*The Diary of a Young Girl,*
by Anne Frank, May 3, 1944

"If all men are good at heart, there never really was an Auschwitz; nor is there any possibility that it may recur."

—"The Ignored Lesson of Anne Frank,"
by Bruno Bettelheim, in *Anne Frank: Reflections on Her Life and Legacy,* edited by Hyman A. Enzer and Sandra Solotaroff-Enzer

THIRTEEN

I HAD KNOWN THERE WOULD be a movie. How could there not be? The play won a Pulitzer Prize. All over America, every night, road-company Ottos stumbled into stage set annexes to discover their daughters' diaries, and Annes and Peters fell in love, and a dozen different versions of my father, tall, short, fat, thin, stole bread out of my mouth. All over the world. In Amsterdam, the Queen attended a performance and was moved, and commoners emerged from the theater uplifted. They were not Nazis. They had tried to save their Jews. Never mind that they had had fewer to begin with and had given up more of them proportionately than any other country. In Germany, theatergoers expressed their shock and dismay. If only they had known what was going on, they would have spoken out. One woman was so deeply affected by Anne's plight she insisted that particular little Jewess, at least, should have been permitted to live. Others identified with the hardships they saw on the stage. They too had suffered under their Führer. But a play can reach only so many people. A movie is a phenomenon of a different dimension. Hollywood would be morally remiss if it did not put Anne's diary on film.

No matter where I turned, I found stories about the movie. The actor Joseph Schildkraut would repeat his role as Otto. The Nazi actress would play Mrs. Frank again. So much for the outrage of my wife and thousands of other right-thinking people. But there would be a new Anne. A new Peter too, but that was of less importance. The star search for the new Anne was the big news. Read all about it. What fortunate young miss would win the sweepstakes? Who would be lucky enough to be Anne Frank?

The same comedy team who had turned Pfeffer into a bumbling clown and my father into a thief—I am sorry to keep bringing that up, but I still do not understand how they got away with it—would write the screenplay, but the director, a man called George Stevens, was known for more serious films. He had been with the American troops when they liberated Dachau, so he knew his stuff, the papers said. He also had a reputation for realism. In matters of verisimilitude, money was no object for George Stevens and the gentlemen at 20th Century Fox. When bombs fell on the secret annex in the movie, I read, Mr. Stevens would not hit the camera to make it tremble, as most directors would do. Instead he had a special set built on wooden pillars and springs. At the appropriate moment, workmen shook the contraption and frightened the living daylights out of the actors. I was interested in the details of the construction. After all, I am a builder. But I was not persuaded it would have the same effect as the RAF. Mr. Stevens also insisted that Miss Shelley Winters, the actress playing Mrs. van Daan, gain forty pounds. I did not remember my mother's being overweight, but perhaps that was because by the end we were all starving. But Miss Winters, the papers reported, was a good sport and a true professional. She was eating her way into my mother's character, like a tapeworm.

When Madeleine told me she would go to the movie with her sister, I knew she had not forgotten my outburst the evening she had come home from the play. Wives took the train to New York and went to theater matinees without their husbands. They did not go to the local movie houses without us. If one of them did, she better have a good reason.

"I know you don't want to see it." She kept her eyes down as she spoke, not because she was avoiding my gaze, but because she was concentrating on the cake she was baking. She called it baking, though it required no cooking other than melting some chocolate. It was a concoction made by pouring the chocolate over ladyfingers, which she bought in the supermarket, then sticking the whole thing in the refrigerator for a few hours. It was tasty enough, but it was not what I would call a real cake, though perhaps I have been spoiled by years of too little nourishment and too much imagination. I remembered when food was the stuff of storytelling, the substance of myth. My mother's babka, we whispered to one another, my grandmother's strudel, my wife's goulash, and our mouths watered and eyes teared, though we were dehydrated as well as starving, and who knew where the secretions came from.

"What makes you say I don't want to see it?"

"Your reaction to the play."

"I had no reaction to the play. I didn't even see the play."

She did not answer immediately. She was having difficulty getting the ladyfingers to stand up around the side of the metal spring pan.

"To tell you the truth," she said, as she wedged the last ladyfinger in—it is a phrase I dislike; why should she begin a sentence by swearing honesty?—"I'm not even sure I want to see it. But I will."

"Why would you go to a movie you don't want to see?"

She took the saucepan of melted chocolate from the burner and began spooning it over the ladyfingers. "It's a moral obligation."

"A moral obligation?"

She looked up from the pseudo-cake. "People like me, people who have had it easy, have no right to close their eyes."

I should have kept my mouth shut. That was a trait on which I prided myself. If I had to say something, I should have told her not to be silly. Going to a movie had no moral implications. But the conviction that burned in her eyes when she talked about not closing them was infuriating. I don't know why. I had married her for her blindness.

"In the DP camp, I was assigned to work in the hospital for a while."

She stood, the saucepan suspended in midair, her eyes focused not on some distant moral imperative, but on me. I never talked about my past. She did not want to miss a word.

"There was a man, half his face had been blown away. I think he had stepped on a mine."

I saw her flinch. I really should have stopped.

"At least that was the story. Who knew what was what under the bandages? His head was swathed in them. All that was left were two holes for his eyes. His eyes were okay. Except for the lids. He had no eyelids."

A spot of chocolate spattered to the counter. She put down the saucepan. I warned myself to stop.

"Without eyelids," I went on, "he could not close his eyes. Obviously."

She was still staring at me. She had no idea what I was getting at. How could she?

"You know what happens if you can't close your eyes?"

"You can't sleep?"

"No, you can sleep with your eyes open. Many people do." I had lived in enough unholy barracks to know that. "If you don't have eyelids, you cannot stop crying. If you can't close your eyes, you cry all the time."

This time I did not apologize. I was too angry. She had made me break my vow of silence. To a man like me, the only honor left, the only decency possible, is to protect others from the horror.

MADELEINE DID not talk about the movie when she got home, though I knew she was thinking about it. For the next few days, she moved through the upholstered and buffed rooms of the house with an air of tender distraction. It was more than sorrow for the poor bastards she had seen impersonated on the screen. It was longing. She wanted to know what it was like to suffer, for a while.

MY WIFE had watched the movie in the big theater in the new shopping center a few minutes from Indian Hills. I had to drive half an hour to see it.

The green spring afternoon was shot with sunlight. It was not a day to be sitting in a dark movie house. I told Madeleine I had to go to the office, then stop by the site. I even drove to the office. I pulled into the parking lot, then pulled out again and kept going down the highway. According to the schedule in the paper, I had just enough time.

The theater was filled with children and old people. I was the only grown man in his prime willing to while away the afternoon so fecklessly. I took a seat on the aisle. I did not want to bother people when I left. I had no intention of staying till the end. I was merely curious to see a few minutes of it.

I had to sit through three or four coming attractions before the movie started. My foot tapped the soft-drink-slicked floor. I was not nervous. I merely wanted to get on with it.

The name of the studio took shape on the screen. The air swelled with what sounded like several hundred strings. Cloud-white letters shimmering against an open sky. *The Diary of Anne Frank*. She would have liked that. The camera panned from the sky to the Westerkerk to the canal. My head spun for a moment, but that was only vertigo induced by the shot. A truck full of refugees, some of them still in striped uniforms, rolled down the street. Joseph Schildkraut lumbered down from it. I had to hand it to the actor. Not only did he look like

Otto—the resemblance was uncanny—he even moved like
him. A lesser actor would have hunched himself into a question mark of misery, but Schildkraut had obviously studied
Otto. He moved like a man whose spirit was broken but whose
bearing, thanks to the German army, was still straight.

One after another, the characters appeared on the screen. I
had to smile. The milkily lovely actress—a former model, I had
read—bore no relation to anyone I had known, but then perhaps moviegoers do not want to pay good money to see a girl
with uneven teeth and a shadow of soft down on her upper lip.
There was a boy called Peter. He was clean-cut and athletic, but
with what is called a sensitive side. I felt a flash of envy, though
I could not say whether it was for the golden boy on the screen
or the storybook character he was playing. Shelley Winters
lifted her skirt, and cavorted around the set, and shook her
bleached blond curls. I wished they had not made her a
bleached blonde. Her husband snarled and grumbled from
under a bristly black mustache. Dussel, the dentist, joined the
group, and the story took a comic twist. The writers had cre-
ated an amusing idiot. I could not help laughing. The whole
audience was chuckling at Dussel's foolishness and Anne's eye-
rolling, sweet-smiling triumphs over him, and I was laughing
harder than anyone, so hard that the thick-necked woman in
the seat in front of me turned around to give me a dirty look. I
apologized, but a minute later I was laughing again. I could not
help myself. She turned around again and said if I could not
restrain myself, I ought to leave and let others enjoy the show. I
managed to calm down then. I had no desire to call attention
to myself. Besides, the bombing scene had started, and I did
not want to miss that. I was curious to see if Mr. Stevens's set

worked. I am sorry to say that he did not get his money's worth. I could tell that even without knowing the cost of labor and supplies. The scene was a child's idea of a bombing, or an American civilian's.

The boy called Peter stopped snapping at Anne, and Anne stopped playing practical jokes on him, and they began to give each other ardent looks. Anne climbed the stairs to his room, and the parents worried and argued about it, but it was a clean-cut American movie with clean-cut American kids, even if they were supposed to be German Jews hiding in Amsterdam, and, unlike the parents, everyone in the audience knew there was nothing to worry about, at least when it came to sex. When they finally kissed, the girl beside me sighed achingly.

I glanced at my watch. The movie was longer than I had anticipated. When I looked back up at the screen, it was dark except for a single flickering flame. There was shouting and scuffling. Thief! Thief! Mrs. Frank screams. Bread out of the mouths of children, she wails. I have heard your own son moaning in his sleep from hunger, she howls. Otto steps forward and speaks.

"We don't need the Nazis to destroy us. We're destroying ourselves."

"For God's sake," I muttered.

The woman in front of me turned again.

"I'm sorry," I whispered, but Otto should have known better. Anybody who had been through what Otto had should have known better than to speak a line like that. Then I remembered, Otto was not saying the line, the actor was. Otto had never spoken the line, because we had never had the fight, because my father had never stolen the bread.

It was almost over now. I knew that from the siren, though there had been no siren when the Green Police came. But I understood why the director inserted the effect. The shriek of the siren sawed across my nerves, though I had not heard it in years. The girl next to me, who had probably never heard it, began to sob. When the police shattered the glass of the front door, something else they had not done, the thick-necked woman in front of me moaned. The darkness vibrated with the sounds of whimpers and groans and honking noses.

The camera panned back to the sky. Clouds swirled overhead. Gulls shrieked and swooped. The movie was over, but it was not quite the end. There were Westerbork and Auschwitz and Bergen-Belsen to come. There were even scenes of that, but they had ended up on the cutting room floor. I had read somewhere that the director had shot a final scene in a make-believe Auschwitz, but the audiences in the sneak previews had scrawled outrage on their opinion cards. The Anne they knew and loved had not died in a concentration camp. At least, they did not want to see her die in a concentration camp.

The thin singsong voice of the milky-skinned actress floated out over the discarded candy wrappers and crushed popcorn boxes and people already shuffling up the aisle toward the light.

In spite of everything, I still believe people are good at heart.

A sigh shuddered through the theater. That was what the audience wanted. The triumph of the human spirit, as my wife called it. The reassurance that in spite of everything, of people going to their deaths by the millions merely for the accident of their birth, of other people willing and eager to pry gold fillings from their mouths before they shoveled them into ovens, of ghoulish experiments on unanesthetized individuals in the interest of medical science, of an entire people's bloodthirsty complicity to cleanse the world of another entire people, in spite of all that, human beings are good at heart.

Nonetheless, I was glad I had seen the movie, despite the inane last line. I had finally got it out of my system.

"Lou Jacobi is irksomely sluggish and pathetically lax as the weakling van Daan."
—A review of the movie *The Diary of Anne Frank* by Bosley Crowther

"Is it necessary that Mrs. v. Daan calls me 'a saint'? I understand that you want to sketch her as hysterical and exaggerating, but I feel a little ashamed."
—Otto Frank in notes for the playwrights

FOURTEEN

■ ■ MADELEINE HAD PROPPED THE BIG photograph against
■ ■ the wall in the living room with a kitchen towel tucked behind the blond wood frame so it would not scratch the wall. I had helped choose the picture, but this was the first time I had seen the finished product.

"It turned out well," she said. "Don't you think?"

"Very well," I agreed.

We stood side by side staring at the framed portrait. Our three children stared back at us. The photographer had come to the house several weeks earlier. It had not been an easy afternoon, Madeleine said. David had been cranky. Betsy was getting a cold. Choosing among the proofs had been almost as difficult. If it was a good likeness of Abigail, Betsy's eyes were closed. When Betsy was at her best, David was sulking. We had finally settled on one that almost did justice to all three, though it did not capture Betsy's spirit. She was feisty, my middle child, and though she could drive Madeleine and me wild with frustration, I was glad. I did not want any of my children to be too docile. Not that I was looking for troublemakers. I was hoping they would know when to put up a struggle and when to hang back in the shadows. I wanted them to be canny.

In the photograph, they sat in size places, David leaning against Betsy, Abigail with an arm around Betsy's shoulders. The frame had worked out well too. Madeleine had spent half an afternoon in the shop choosing it. Now all I had to do was hang the portrait above the sofa.

I put my arm around Madeleine's waist as I went on staring at my three American children, scrubbed, well fed, smiling into the camera as if happiness were their birthright. I am not superstitious, but standing there looking at that picture, I understood peasant women who tie red ribbons on their children to ward off the evil eye and primitives who speak of their offsprings' ugliness in loud voices to fool jealous gods.

"Handsome little devils, aren't they?" Madeleine said.

I wanted to tell her to speak more softly.

"I'm glad I decided to let Abigail wear that dress."

A red ribbon would not have detracted from it.

"What I want to know is where David got that hair," she said. "Not from either of us. You're lighter than I am, but neither of us is fair enough to have a towheaded son."

"My mother had blond hair."

Madeleine looked up at me in surprise. "You never told me that," she said, as if I told her anything about my parents.

I shrugged.

"I wish they could have known their grandparents," she went on, turning back to the photograph. "For the obvious reasons, of course, but something else too. I have the feeling, I know it's silly, I never even met your parents, but I have the feeling another set of grandparents, a different kind of grandparents, would have made the children, I don't know, less parochial."

I did not answer. I was too busy thinking about my mother's hair. It had been dark brown, streaked with gray the last time I saw her. I could not imagine where the comment about her being blond had come from, but I would not retract it now.

I HAD mistaken the color of my mother's hair. That was not a criminal offense. Years pass. Memories fade. Thank heavens. Perhaps it would have been different if I had had photographs, though even they lie. I remember a picture taken in the school-yard in Osnabrück, a row of eight- and nine-year-old boys standing in a line, each with arms around the shoulders of the boys on either side of him. I am in the center, one of the tallest of the group, the strongest-looking, the one with the mean expression. If you look at that picture, you will say, what a bully. But I was not the bully in that photograph. The other boys had been taunting me. Jew, they called me. Yid. Christ-killer. That is why I look so mean. Because I know I am going to cry. But I will not cry. I will not give them the satisfaction. And I did not. Or did I? How can I be sure?

■ ■ ■ ■

IT HAPPENED again a week later at Madeleine's parents' house. It was a Sunday afternoon. Susannah and Norman were there too. We were sitting around the dinner table, and the children were running in and out of the dining room, and there was nothing unusual about the situation. Even the conversation was familiar. My mother-in-law was trying to persuade my father-in-law to shave his mustache.

"Look at Norman," she said.

We all turned to look at my brother-in-law.

"You see how nice and smooth he looks."

"Like a baby's tush," my father-in-law said.

"Even Peter," my mother-in-law went on, clearly scraping the bottom of the clean-shaven barrel. My father-in-law loves me like a son. My mother-in-law still regards me as the thief who stole her daughter from a more worthy suitor. Perhaps larceny runs in my family. "You don't see him with hair on his face."

"I'm too old to change," my father-in-law insisted.

"Don't say that, Daddy," Susannah said. "Besides, that's Mommy's point." My wife and her sister still call their parents by the terms of childhood. I thought they would stop when they had children of their own, but I was wrong. "You'd look younger without a mustache."

"You see, Susannah agrees," my mother-in-law said. "You get rid of that gray mustache, you lose five years. Maybe ten. Am I right, Norman?"

"Five years, definitely," Norman said.

"And if he did shave it off," Madeleine said, "if he walked in one night without it, you'd be screaming who's that stranger in my house."

The moment Susannah took her mother's side, I knew Madeleine would espouse her father's. The constantly shifting alliances in my wife's family still amaze me. They disagree and conspire and jockey among themselves as if there is no tomorrow, or as if they are sure there will be one. It never occurs to them that there might not be enough time to make amends.

"What about you, Pete?" my father-in-law asked. "You're the only one hasn't rung in on the subject."

They all turned to me. I was a member of the family, even if I was not exactly one of them.

"I admire a mustache," I said.

My mother-in-law shot a look down the table. I have often thought she would make an excellent military officer.

"My father had a mustache," I went on.

My father had not had a mustache, any more than my mother had been a blonde. The long mournful face that could twist into humor, or rage, in a moment had been hairless from the top of his high balding forehead to his prominent chin.

We were in the car on the way home, when I realized where I had got the idea. Lou Jacobi, the actor in the movie, the one who steals the bread, had a mustache. It was black and bristly and a little like Hitler's, come to think of it.

THE INCIDENT that afternoon on the site was of no importance, though at the time it gave me a scare. I thought I was losing my vision, just as years ago I had lost my voice.

I was walking through one of the unfinished houses. It was

almost five, and the workmen had left, but Harry was supposed to meet me there. In the distance, a stand of trees,
etched black against the pale sheet of late afternoon sky,
caught my attention. The trees made the raw earth around me
look even more barren. The first thing we did when we moved
onto a piece of land was bulldoze everything in sight. I did not
like to do it, but I had stopped fighting Harry some time ago.
You would be surprised how little people care. As long as they
have a kitchen with countertop range and wall oven, a bathroom with twin sinks, and a family room with floor-to-ceiling
sliding glass doors, they do not care what they see when they
look through those doors. They do not care if they have
mimosas or chestnuts or oaks or a gouged wasteland to look at.
The only reason the stand in the distance had been spared was
because it was not on our property.

The trees in the distance reminded me of the park at the end
of the Hunzestraat, the one near the flat where we had lived
before we disappeared. That was the way our Christian neighbors would have thought of it, no questions asked. The less
you knew about others, the better. Before the decree forbidding Jews to enter public parks for fear their uncleanliness
would contaminate the benches, my parents had liked to stroll
there. I stood in the half-finished house and saw my mother
and father walking beneath the distant trees. They were coming
toward me slowly, her hand tucked into the angle made by his
arm, his long scarecrow's body listing toward hers. As they
drew closer, I recognized the cigarette drooping from his
mouth. She was wearing her good black hat with the grosgrain
ribbon and jaunty narrow brim. They made their way toward
me through the mosaic of light and shadow till we were stand-

ing only inches apart. My father's face was on a level with mine, though I could not see his features. The smoke was too thick for that. He tipped his head back, opened his mouth, and let out a perfect ring. That was the father I remembered.

I turned to my mother. She was shorter than my father and me, and I could not see her face beneath the brim of the hat. I bent my knees and twisted my body to look under it. The sight pushed me back against the raw wooden struts. It was something out of a horror movie. My mother's face was a blob of blank white flesh. She had no features. She was nothing.

I slid to the unfinished floor and sat with my back against the struts, legs drawn up, face resting on my knees, arms crossed over my head. It was the posture we used to assume when we cowered beneath the falling bombs.

"Hey, pal."

The words came to me through the explosions going off in my head.

"Are you okay?"

He pried my arms loose from my head.

"Are you okay, pal?"

I opened my eyes. The purple-shadowed jaw, the too-close-together eyes, the bald head beneath a few combed-across strands of dark hair filled my vision. I had never been so happy to see Harry's unhandsome face. I was not going blind after all.

I DID not make a habit of going to the safe in the closet to count the money I had stashed there. I was not a miser. Nor was I Verfolgungsbedingt, that noxious German word for that sad pathological condition. I merely found it reassuring, every so often, to make sure that things were in order. You never knew when an emergency would arise. The vision of my parents strolling in the Hunzestraat had reminded me of that. And since I was having trouble falling asleep, I decided I might as well use the time productively. There was no point in lying in bed, imagining mayhem in the moving shadows the tree outside the window made on the ceiling. If I faced the night table, the glowing hands of the clock, inching forward, jangled my nerves. If I turned the other way, the sight of my wife, sleeping as I could not, irritated me. She lay on her side, her knees drawn up, her back to me. I lifted the covers gently. Her skin was waxy in the dim moonlight. Her spine made a delicate outline beneath it. How easily it would snap. I could almost hear the sound of it breaking. I smoothed the covers over her, climbed out of bed, and made my way out of the room. I was careful to close the door before I switched on the hall light. The clean-laundry smell was bracing. The numbers clicked into place. The door swung open.

I took out the passport and checked the expiration date. I knew it by heart, but I liked to see it in black and white. I have not got where I am by being careless. I returned it to the safe and drew out the manila envelopes. There were two of them now. I did not want big bills. I opened the first envelope. The twenties, fifties, and hundreds, not suspiciously crisp and new, but reassuringly worn, were sorted by denomination and held together by rubber bands. I went through the piles, slipping off the bands, counting the bills, making a mental note of the tally, replacing the rubber band, and going on to the next. Everything added up properly. I put the bundles back in the envelope, fastened the flap, and opened the second one. It contained the same amount. I had divided the bills evenly. I began counting. When I finished, I was a hundred and seventy dollars short. I started over. This time I was missing two hundred and twenty. I did not understand it. No one else knew the combination to the safe. I still had not got around to giving it to Madeleine, though I swore I would do it first thing in the morning. I went through the money a third time. Now I was three hundred over what should have been there. This was insane. I am not bad with figures, but I could not make these bills add up. I went downstairs to the kitchen. I did not want to risk going back to the bedroom and waking Madeleine. I took a pad from the small desk in the corner and a pencil from the cup Abigail had made in school, and climbed to the upstairs hall again. The sight of the open linen closet, towels jumbled, safe yawning, gave me a start. I knew it had not been ransacked. The disorder was my doing. But that was the way it looked. I took out the envelope that refused to add up, closed the safe, and spun the lock. I even straightened the towels and closed the closet door. I wanted to be able to concentrate on counting the bills, and the sight of the seemingly looted safe was disturbing.

I sat on the floor under the overhead light with the envelope, pencil, and pad. I knew it was foolish. The money could not have gone anywhere. The fact that I got a different sum each time meant the fault was mine. But I had to make it come out right. If I could not count on this, what could I count on?

I began the tally again. This time I wrote down the amount of each bundle after I counted it. I had gone through three stacks of twenties and one of fifties when the door to the girls' bedroom opened. Abigail stood in the framed rectangle. The darkness behind her outlined her white nightgown and sleep-pale face. She was a ghostly photographic negative of herself.

She blinked against the light and rubbed an eye with one fist. "Water," she said, and the word opened into a yawn.

I stood, and we went together into the bathroom, her sleep-tangled hair brushing my pajamas as she leaned against me. At the sink, she lifted her head to drink from the plastic glass rimmed with daisies, and her Adam's apple pulsed like a heart-beat. She wiped her mouth with the back of her hand, and we started back across the hall. Her small pink feet crackled the bills I had left on the carpet. She looked down at them.

"What's that?"

I stood gazing at her upturned face. It was sleepy but inquisitive. She was old enough to know. Children younger than she had survived on their own. I sat on the floor, took her hand, and pulled her down beside me.

"It's money," I explained. "Money I put away in case we ever have to run."

The eyes she turned up to me were crusted with sleep. "Run?"

"Leave here. Go someplace else."

"Why?"

"Sometimes people have to. This is to make sure that if we have to, Mommy and you and Betsy and David and me, all of us together, we can. My daddy didn't think ahead, but I have. So you don't have to be afraid."

"Of what?"

"Anything."

She picked up a hundred-dollar bill and sat staring at it dumbly.

"Do you want to help me count it?"

Her head drooped forward. I took it as an assent.

"Come on. I'll count, and you write down the numbers."

Her head slumped against my shoulder. I put the pencil in her hand.

"We'll have to start over. I lost track when I got up." I arranged the piles of money in neat rows, took the first stack of hundreds, and slipped off the rubber band. Her head drooped lower against my arm. "Come on, it'll be fun."

She lifted her head. I began counting. "Three thousand," I said when I finished the first stack. I had to shake her gently to get her to write the number on the pad. "Write a three and three zeros." As I picked up another bundle of bills, I heard the door open behind me.

"What are you doing?" Madeleine's bare feet were beside me on the carpet. She swooped down and picked up a bundle of bills. "What on earth are you doing?"

"I was thirsty," Abigail said. My firstborn was loyal, or perhaps she simply misunderstood her mother and thought the anger was directed at her.

"She got up for a glass of water, and I thought it would be fun for her to help me."

"Fun for her to help you! Count money? At one-thirty in the morning? Are you out of—" She stopped and stood looking down at me. I said nothing. I was not going to defend myself for taking care of her and the children.

She reached down, took Abigail's hand, and drew her to her feet. "Come on, sweetie, back to bed."

I was still on the floor with the piles of money when

Madeleine came out of the girls' room and closed the door behind her.

"I'll be finished in a minute," I told her, before she could say anything.

She crossed the hall, went into our bedroom, and closed that door without a word. I was sorry she was annoyed, but I had to get the money to come out correctly. I started from the beginning again. This time it all added up.

THE NEXT evening I brought Madeleine a dozen roses. She thanked me, and said they were beautiful, and asked me to get the tall vase down from the top cabinet for them. I was relieved. I had been afraid she would be brooding about the night before, though I still could not see what was wrong with a man trying to take care of his family.

While she ran water into the vase and arranged the flowers, I turned to the pile of mail she had been going through when I walked in. It was the usual assortment, a few bills, a flyer from a carpet-cleaning establishment and another from an exterminator, a letter from the local chapter of a Jewish organization thanking me for my contribution. Even that was not out of the ordinary. I made donations to Catholic Charities and the Boy Scouts, the United Fund and the United Jewish Appeal, to name only a few, and the various recipients sent back letters thanking me for my generosity. This particular letter also told me about the good deeds my money would effect and wished me and my family G-D's blessings. As I stood staring down at the letter, I understood Madeleine's high spirits.

The first time I saw the eviscerated word was in a newsletter lying on a table in Madeleine's parents' house, though at the time I still thought of it as Susannah's parents' house. It was the moment, Madeleine would tell me later, when she knew that Susannah would never marry me, and she would.

"What's this?" I asked, pointing to one of the scores of G-dash-Ds scattered over the page.

"God," Susannah said.

It could not be a typographical error. It occurred too often. "Then why don't they just write it?"

"You're not supposed to spell out the word."

"Why aren't you supposed to spell out the word?" I wasn't arguing with her. I was curious.

"It's blasphemy."

"It's blasphemy if you say goddamn. It's not blasphemy if"—I glanced down at one sentence—"you're writing about being grateful to God."

"That's just the way it is," Susannah insisted.

"That's not an answer," Madeleine said. Until then I had forgotten she was in the room. In those days, Susannah had that effect on me.

I turned from her to Madeleine. She shook her head in annoyance at herself. "All my life I've been reading G-dash-D, and I never even thought about it. Even after Anthropology 101, I didn't think about it. But now you make me see how absurd it is."

I was sorry I had said anything. Susannah could write God backward and upside down, for all I cared. Spelling was not what I was after.

"What does Anthropology 101 have to do with it?" Susannah asked.

"Explain it to her, Peter."

I did not have to explain it to Susannah. She knew what her sister and I were driving at. Superstition and primitive practices and graven images. The words, suspended in the air, waiting to be plucked from it, frightened Susannah. They intrigued Madeleine. The fact that I had summoned them thrilled her. That was why she had not objected to the flowers I had brought her. Last night, she had come out of the bedroom and stumbled upon a husband whose universe was shrinking to the size of a one-foot-square wall safe. This evening, she had opened a letter and rediscovered a boy who had promised, and threatened, a larger world. The memory must have had a gasp of life in it still, because as she passed me on her way to the living room to put the vase of roses in the bay window, she went up on her toes to kiss me in thanks, or maybe for no reason at all.

I HAD been right to bring Madeleine flowers the day after she caught me counting money with Abigail, but I came home empty-handed the following week. This time she did not tell me not to bring her anything, but I knew.

The girls were never in danger, no matter what she said, though I suppose I should not have left them alone in the car. But if I dashed into Korvettes for the roll of film on my own, I could be back in three minutes. If I had them in tow, it would take at least half an hour. Betsy would try to drag me toward the aisles lined with plastic toys, and Abigail would come to a covetous halt in front of the cheap jewelry. It would be easier to dash in, grab the film, and be back in a minute. They were not infants. It was broad daylight.

I found a space two rows down from the entrance, told them I would be right back, got out of the car, and started across the parking lot. Inside, I headed straight for the film. There were no other customers at the counter. I was on my way out the door before I knew it. I stopped only long enough to hold it for a woman with two toddlers in tow. How could I not?

The rest of the story is so foolish I am ashamed to remember it. It was a comedy, really. The kind of thing Dussel the fool would do, if the playwrights transported him to the suburbs of America. Dussel would lose his wits in the big sprawling parking lot of the new E. J. Korvettes, and the audience would laugh, and it would all work out in the end, as it did. But I am not a fool like Dussel, and I would not have lost my wits that afternoon, if it were not for the girls. Madeleine was wrong when she accused me of irresponsibility. Actually, she used a stronger word than that, but she was upset and did not know what she was saying. If I had not been worried sick about the girls, I would not have gone half crazy when I misplaced the car, and the rest would never have happened.

I started across the parking lot. You had to hand it to the company. It was not just the discounts, it was the ease. There must have been room for eight hundred, maybe a thousand cars. I sprinted down the row looking for my Cadillac. Harry had finally won me over. I was halfway to the end of the line before I realized I was in the wrong row. I cut through the parked cars, and started up the next aisle.

The rest is an old story. It happens every day. People come out of a different door from the one they entered, misplace their cars, and wander around cursing their own stupidity until they find it. I did a lot of cursing that afternoon. I also did a lot of running, up one row, down the other. I stopped at every maroon car, even the ones that were not Cadillacs. I peered into every dark Cadillac. None of them had two little girls inside.

I stopped running and stood for a minute. The sun pressed down on my head like a steel helmet. Sweat stung my eyes. I took off my dark glasses to wipe them. The light glinting off shiny bumpers and bright hoods was blinding. I put my glasses back on.

I had to remain calm. My daughters were here, somewhere, safe in the car. I tried to remember if I had left the windows open. But they were not infants. If they were too hot, they would roll down a window. Except the car had those new push-button windows. I saw my two little girls sprawled lifeless across the seats. In the heat and glare, the image wavered into thousands of lifeless little-girl bodies strewn over a gray landscape. I started to run again.

A police car cruised by. I raised my arm to hail it, then caught sight of the men inside. Their faces were pitiless masks. In place of eyes, they had flat silver disks that shot sunlight. I imagined the guns strapped to their brutal sides. I dropped my hand and started to run again.

I could feel the big breakfast Madeleine had made me rising in my chest. I spat out a mouthful of saliva. The taste of stale bacon grease coated my mouth. I spat again. I felt my knees begin to buckle and grabbed the hood of a car for support, but I could not control my insides. My body convulsed. My breakfast spewed out. I felt like the fools who, when the camps were liberated, had refused to listen to reason and stuffed themselves with food their bodies could not accept.

The car stopped beside me. I turned to face it. From under

peaked caps, four silver disks glared at me. One of the cops had a handlebar mustache. It trembled around his words. "You okay, sir?"

The sir did not fool me. I told him I was fine.

"Sure you don't need any help?"

I shook my head back and forth. I was afraid if I opened my mouth to speak, I would throw up again, or tell them to stay the hell out of my business.

The cop with the mustache looked at the one behind the wheel. The driver shrugged. The car purred off.

I waited until it was out of sight to start running again. Only after I covered the entire lot in what I always think of as the front of the building did I remember there was another lot in the back. My daughters were where I had left them, a little way down the second row.

"You were in there forever." Betsy dragged out the last word.

I told them about getting mixed up. I made it sound like a joke. Wasn't daddy silly? They thought it was hilarious. Guess what Daddy did, they burst into the house shouting. That was how Madeleine found out about it. I would not have been foolish enough to tell her myself.

THE NEXT incident was even more absurd. It never would have happened if it had not been for those damn cops cruising the Korvettes parking lot the week before. You okay? they asked, as if they gave a damn. Sir, they called me, as if they wouldn't throw me into a stinking cell at the drop of a hat, or an order from above, or just for fun.

I know what I sound like, but I am not Verfolgungsbedingt. If I were, would I have built a successful company, and raised a family, and become a pillar of the community? The National Association of Home Builders does not give awards to men haunted by the past. I do not condemn those poor souls for their problems. I wish them every aid and compensation, though what can compensate for such acts I cannot imagine. But I am not one of them.

I was alone in the house with David that afternoon. That is another thing. You do not leave a baby alone with someone about whom you can use the term Verfolgungsbedingt. Madeleine never would have gone out with the girls and left me with David, if I had been behaving dangerously. I would not have let her, if I thought I might hurt him.

David was upstairs napping. I was sitting at the kitchen table with a glass of iced coffee left over from lunch and the *Times* crossword puzzle. People with the kind of symptoms judged Verfolgungsbedingt do not do crossword puzzles either. I had started doing them recently, though I had not looked at one since those endless hours in the annex. No doubt my old friend Gabor would make something of that. He would be wrong. I simply had more time these days. That was also the reason I had taken down the diary and reread it. That, and the fact that I wanted to make sure there was nothing in it about my father's stealing bread. There was not, of course. The absence was reassuring. The movie would fade. It was not even in the theaters anymore. The play would die. All those European companies could not go on forever. If anything endured, it would be the book. The view of a thirteen-year-old girl might not be as reliable as the *Encyclopedia Britannica,* but it was not the pack of lies the play and movie had fashioned.

One sequence in the book did disturb me, though. It was the night I neglected to unbolt the door, so that the next morning Kugler and the workmen could not get in. I had put the incident out of my mind. It was unimportant. It had not given us away. But now it had come back. Sometimes, when I was sitting in a meeting or driving down the highway, I could hardly keep from groaning at the memory. One night when I went down to lock up the house on Seminole Road, I saw the accusing faces of the inhabitants of the annex staring back at me from the dark windows.

"I'm sorry," I muttered. "I meant to unlock it. I thought I had unlocked it."

"What did you say?" Madeleine called from the upstairs hall.

I told her I had not spoken. It was the television, which we had neglected to turn off.

The heavy brass knocker thudded against the front door. I lifted my head from the crossword puzzle. No one in Indian Hills used front doors. People came up the driveway, through the garage, and into the family room. The morning I forgot to unbolt the door, Kugler did not bang on it either. No one was supposed to be inside. He went next door and broke the glass to the kitchen window in the office. Who was to say someone had not seen him? Just because no one came that morning did not mean I was not guilty of giving us away the night before. The Green Police had not pounded on the door, but banging on the door was what we were expecting. The director of the movie was right about that. At night, in our sleep, we dreamed the noise. During the day, we imagined it. Shh, we said. What was that? we asked one another. Did you hear something at the door?

The brass knocker sounded again. I was glad Madeleine and the girls were not home. I only hoped she would see the truck on the street from a distance and have the sense to turn back or keep going past. I should have drilled her. I had gone over it in my mind again and again, but I never told her what to do. I had not wanted to frighten her.

That was ridiculous. No one was hunting us. I was not in hiding. This was a clean, well-maintained, fully-paid-for house in America, not a vermin-infested secret annex on a murky canal in Amsterdam. The refrigerator hummed. The Dutch girl in the shape of a cookie jar smiled. The cat we called Mouschi slept on a chair beside me. Even he was not the real Mouschi, but a cat I had adopted after the play closed, a cat who had been trained to walk across a stage, and knock over a saucer of milk, and do any number of nifty tricks on command. The children were wild about him.

The knocker struck the brass plate again. Mouschi's ears lifted into twin pink-lined triangles. Yellow stars for the Jews, pink triangles for the fairies. Stop it, I warned myself, but I could not help standing. I was careful not to scrape the legs of the chair on the linoleum floor. I crossed the kitchen on tiptoe. When I reached the living room carpet, I stepped over the spot at the bottom of the stairs that always creaks, then hugged the wall on the left to stay out of the line of vision from the long, narrow window next to the door.

I had to stoop to look out the peephole. From under a peaked cap, a white face, the features squashed wide and flat and vicious by the distorting glass of the tiny opening, stared back at me. I could not make out the insignia on the cap. It did not matter. The last time they had come in civilian suits, except for the one who had dumped Anne's diary out of the briefcase and stuffed the money and jewelry into it. He was the only one in uniform. The rough green fabric was slimy with dirt. Even the Green Police were short of soap by that time.

I went on peering through the peephole. This uniform was blue. A new division. Old tricks in new uniforms.

He lifted his hand. The peephole turned dark. The door vibrated against my face as he brought the knocker down. I jumped back.

I would have preferred to go down to the basement. My workbench was well stocked with hammers and saws and heavy tools. I had carried a hammer when I went downstairs to find the burglar with my father and Otto. I had used an axe in the barn. But I did not have time to go to the basement.

Hugging the wall again, I returned to the kitchen and ducked across it to the drawer next to the sink where Madeleine keeps the bread and carving and other serious knives. The carving knife would go in easily, but the ragged edge of the bread knife would be more effective. I took one in each hand, just to be safe. On my way back to the living room, I was careful to step around the squeaky spot again.

He was standing at the bottom of the two steps now, staring toward the garage. I had left the door open the night before. He could see the car. He knew I was in here. David and I both. Goddammit, would I never learn? I should have closed the garage. Just as I should have unlocked the door to the annex for Kugler and the workmen to get in.

He climbed the steps to the door again. The closer he got, the more misshapen his face grew. This one would want more than money and jewelry. This one was a killer.

He lifted his hand again. This time it didn't cut off my view. I saw it move to the bell. The noise sizzled through the house. The sound died. The house held its breath. The man lifted his arm again, but before he could press the bell, another sound split the silence. My son howled in protest.

I took the stairs two at a time and burst into his room. My son lay on his back in the crib, arms and legs boxing the air, chest heaving like a small earthquake, mouth open to let out his outrage.

"Shh," I pleaded into the crib. "Shh." But he went on howling.

Everyone knew the stories. The mother who put a hand over a child's face to stifle the cry so the SS would not hear, and felt the body go limp in her arms. The father who suffocated a screaming baby to save two older children. But I would not think of the stories.

I hovered over the crib, a knife in each hand. "Be quiet," I hissed.

My son looked up at me. The sound stopped. Sleep-crusted lids blinked over inky blue eyes. I held my breath. He blinked again. I exhaled. He opened his mouth. The sound shook the walls.

I reached into the crib. The light from the window glinted off the carving knife, bright and silvery as a toy. My son's eyes darted to it. His hand reached for it. I pulled it away. He shrieked. The bell rang. The knife dangled over him. He howled and strained his small furious body toward the knife. I pulled it away from him. The bell rang again. Longer this time.

The son-of-a-bitch was leaning on it. David shrieked. I lifted the knife high above the crib.

The bell stopped. My son blinked. His mouth closed. The house shuddered into silence. I sensed something above the crib, a bright sparkling mobile. I looked up and saw the knife in my hand. I pulled my arm back, dropped the knife on the floor, noticed the knife in my other hand, and dropped that too. I reached into the crib and picked up my son. I was still holding him when I heard Madeleine's car pull into the garage. I took both knives in one hand, carried them and David down to the kitchen, and slid them into the drawer, careful to put them back in the same slots. She would never know they had been taken out.

On my way out of the kitchen, I noticed an envelope sticking out from under the front door. Still holding my son, I bent, picked it up, and tore it open. Our local Police Athletic League wanted a contribution.

"I feel wicked sleeping in a warm bed, while somewhere out there my dearest friends are dropping
from exhaustion or being knocked to the ground."
　　　　　　　　　　—The Diary of a Young Girl,
　　　　　　　　by Anne Frank, November 19, 1942

"I've asked myself again and again whether it
wouldn't have been better if we hadn't gone into
hiding if we were dead now and didn't have to go
through this misery."
　　　　　　　　　　—The Diary of a Young Girl,
　　　　　　　　　　by Anne Frank, May 26, 1944

FIFTEEN

■　■ I CAME AWAKE SUDDENLY. On the night table, the
■　■ white hands of the clock carved a slim piece from the
dwindling night. Five-twenty. I turned my head on the pillow.
Madeleine slept as she always did these days, her back to me,
her knees drawn up, her arms holding herself in consolation.
Did she dream of the boy who had walked into her parents'
house speaking languages she did not understand, saying
things the rest of her family shut their ears against, bearing
messages from a larger world she longed to enter? It would be
nice to think there was a realm where I still made her happy.

I lifted the covers. The sight of her spinal cord did not

frighten me. I felt calmer than I had in months. I no longer feared what I might do to her and the children. I knew how to save them from me.

I got out of bed quietly. Inside the closet, I felt for a pair of khakis and slipped into my loafers. At the dresser, I slid open a drawer, took out a polo shirt, and dropped it over my head. I put my car keys and wallet in my pocket, then thought better of it, took out my wallet, removed my driver's license and the small snapshot of the children in the same pose as the large portrait over the sofa, and put them back in my pocket. I would need the license for identification. I wanted the picture of my children. There was only one more thing to do.

I went back to my side of the bed, and in the light from the alarm clock, scrawled a note.

Madeleine dear,
The combination to the safe is eight to the right,
four to the left, six to the right. Kiss the
children for me.

Love, Peter.

I propped the scrap of paper up against the clock. It would be the first thing she saw when she opened her eyes.

THE STATION parking lot was empty. It was too early for commuters. But surely a pre-rush-hour express came through, carrying important people between New York and Philadelphia and Washington. I would not have to wait long.

I pulled into a spot next to the platform and turned off the engine, but left the keys in the ignition. The car was facing east. I had decided on the southbound side. A thin line of gray morning lay on the horizon. The weather forecast had been right. It would be a sticky overcast day. The idea pleased me. Sunshine would have been too cruel. It had been for some time now.

I took the photograph from my pocket. My children stared up at me. They were not smiling as broadly as I had thought when I first saw the picture. Abigail's eyes were shadowed. I had not noticed Betsy's clenched fist. David seemed about to cry. They knew life was no bowl of cherries. I could not keep them safe, but I could protect them from me. I put the photograph back in my pocket and climbed out of the car. Years ago, when I had come here to rid myself of the diary, I had sprinted to the platform, certain that I could outrun my past. I should have known it would catch up with me.

I started toward the steps, my head bent, my shoulders hunched, my feet shuffling. I was walking like an old man. I was walking like my father the last time I had seen him, whichever that was; the time I had done nothing to save him. You think you can wash your hands of your mother and me, he had shouted from the window the night my son was born. The charge had been just, though I had denied it. But I would make amends now. Not that I believed in an afterlife.

I held on to the railing as I dragged myself up the steps to the platform. My legs were heavy. Exhaustion weighed on my shoulders and made my hands tremble. Years ago, the doctor had been wrong about the tremors. They had not been psychosomatic. But he had been right about me. I could not exist on the outside.

I reached the top of the steps and started across the platform. Only once had I taken the train with my children. We were Americans. When we went places, we drove. As we waited on the platform, Abigail had stayed at my side, but Betsy had flirted with danger. She kept edging toward the tracks. Come back here, I had to tell her more than once. Finally, I took her hand in mine and held it tight until the train arrived.

The tracks stretched into the distance like the sutures on a vast wound. I had been in short pants when we took the train from Osnabrück to Amsterdam. The rough plush of the seats had scratched the back of my legs. Stop fidgeting, my father had snapped. His nerves were raw. Was it wise to pull up stakes this way and take his wife, who did not want to go, and child to start over in another country? He was Dutch by birth, but he had lived in Germany all his life. Was it decent to leave his elderly father behind? He was a more dutiful son than I. Stop fidgeting, he had snapped, and my mother had taken the basket down from the overhead rack and produced a piece of her miraculous babka.

There was no babka on the next train, though my father had managed to scavenge a crust of bread that we shared among us. By then he was not agonizing about his decisions, but torturing himself with his mistakes. How had he not seen what was coming? He should have known that forbidding park benches, and decreeing yellow stars, and knocking down old men in the street were only the first measures. But the indignities had progressed to assaults by incremental steps, and he had been lulled. We all had. This is not so bad. Our ancestors suffered harsher affliction. If it gets no worse than this, we can survive. They will come to their senses sooner or later. All we have to do is wait. So we moved from Osnabrück to Amsterdam; and from the flat on the Zuider-Amstellaan, right behind the Franks' on the Merwedeplein, to the annex of 263 Prinsengrcht; and from the annex to the transit camp at Westerbork. And still he tried to fool himself, or maybe only my mother and me. Even when they called our names for the transport east, and everyone knew what that meant, he tried to pretend. Van Pels, the officer shouted when they reached the *p*'s. It was the bark of a mad dog. Hermann. We held our breath. Auguste. My mother began to cry. Peter. At least we will be together, my father said, but he did not look at me when he spoke. He had not saved me, as Pfeffer had saved his son. But then I had not saved him.

I sat on the platform. My legs dangled a few feet above the tracks. It was not much of a jump. Abigail would hesitate, but Betsy would take it easily. I wondered about David. I imagined him at seven, and ten, and thirteen. Would Madeleine have him bar mitzvahed? I did not think so. Her family would pressure her, but she would dig in her heels. She would say Peter would not have wanted it. She would forget the secrets and lies and anger, she would even forget my comment about not wanting David to be mistaken for a Jew, and remember how much I loved her and the children. She would talk to them about me. Daddy said this. Daddy thought that. Daddy would have wanted you to. I would be a better man in myth than I was in life. Like Anne, I would be canonized after my death. It was odd to think that if she had lived, the diary would not have.

It was growing lighter. The oily tracks winked up at me in the gray light. I leaned farther forward and heard the screech of brakes. Women were crying. Men were screaming. Tracks all up and down the area would be tied up for hours. People would

not get to work. Men would miss meetings. Women would forfeit their day of shopping and lunch. It would serve the bastards right, for thinking that was hardship.

I heard the brakes screech again, but this time they were
behind me. A car door slammed.

"Peter!" Madeleine's scream ripped the air. But of course I
was imagining that too. She was still asleep in the dim light of
the luminous clock, muffled by the piece of paper with the
combination to the safe, which I had propped up in front of it.

I put the heels of my hands on the platform, ready to push
myself forward. The arms around my neck were a death grip. I
did not know my wife was so strong. She wrenched my upper
body back. My head hit the platform. She pulled my legs up,
rolled me back from the edge, and flung herself over me. A
strong man could not have pinned me down with as much force.

"What is this?" She shoved the note with the combination
to the safe in my face. "What in hell is this?"

I told her it was the combination to the safe. "In case anything happened to me."

"In case," she shrieked. "In case."

By this time the children had climbed out of the car, though
Madeleine must have told them to stay in the backseat. They
stood at the top of the platform steps, Abigail holding David's
hand, Betsy with her thumb stuck in her mouth, though we had
broken her of the habit years ago. They were shivering in their
summer-weight pajamas. I had wanted to save them from me. I
could not even protect them from a balmy spring morning.

"A man's biography is also history."
—"The American History of Anne Frank's Diary,"
by Judith E. Doneson, in *Anne Frank:*
Reflections on Her Life and Legacy, edited
by Hyman A. Enzer and Sandra Solotaroff-Enzer

SIXTEEN

MADELEINE DID NOT TELL her family about the incident at the railroad station. She was loyal to me. She was also proud in front of them. But she pleaded with me to go back to Dr. Gabor. I told her there was no need. The episode in the station had been an aberration.

"One appointment, Peter. Please. A single hour can't hurt."

"I told you. It won't happen again."

"Just to reassure me."

"It's not necessary."

"For the children, then."

"Goddammit, Madeleine, what are you trying to do? Drive me back to the railroad station?"

Her face crumpled. I had her cornered.

"I don't need Dr. Gabor," I said gently. What I meant was he could not help me. Psychiatry knows no cure for killer instincts.

I could not tuck my daughters in at night for fear of smothering them. I could not lift my son in my arms and spin him around as he screeched with pleasure, because I might lose control and hurl him against a wall. Driving was the worst. Getting behind the wheel of a car with my children in the backseat was riding a roller coaster of murderous panic. My foot weighed numb and heavy on the gas pedal. My arms twitched with the urge to twist the wheel. I saw the car careening into oncoming traffic. I glimpsed it sailing off a bridge. Steel barriers splintered, and air rushed past the windows, and water closed over us. My daughters' hair floated around their stunned faces. My son's small solid legs churned the black water. I struggled to save them, but the current dragged them out of reach. I had thought that night in the barn was an anomaly. Now I knew it was destiny. I had killed once. I would do it again.

YEARS AGO I had said I would return, though at the time I had been sure I was lying. If I had thought about the man with rusty freckles and wiry red hair that might or might not have saved his life, it was only as a mistake I had not made. He was the pedestrian I had swerved in time to avoid hitting, the falling object that had missed me, the banana peel I had not slipped on. His was the world I had refused to enter. He was the man I had not become. So I could not understand what I was doing looking for a parking space on a potholed street in a decaying neighborhood that still, all these years after the war, reeked of paranoia. The early morning sunshine threw every drawn shade and bolted door into sharp relief.

The stone synagogue stood like a hunched old man who has turned his back on the world. I pushed open the door and stepped inside. The clammy air still smelled of rancid food and something equally unpleasant, if less concrete. If I were a romantic, I would have called it despair. I told myself to turn and run while I could. There had been nothing here for me years ago. There was nothing now. I started down the aisle.

The redheaded man was not there. None of the men looked familiar, or rather they all did. Bent under their prayer shawls, trussed up like carcasses in their phylacteries, ancient no matter what their age, they were instantly recognizable for who they were and where they had been. There were eight of them. The number absolved me. Even if I stayed, I would make no difference. They would still be one short of the necessary quorum. Why ten anyway? Why not an even dozen or an easy triumvirate? What biblical sage or Talmudic scholar had determined that God was on the decimal system?

I turned to start back up the aisle. He was coming down it toward me. I had known he would be there. Men like him do not move on.

"So, Mr. Yankee Doodle Dandy," he said as he took my arm, turned me around, and began steering me back down the aisle. "Long time, no see."

He handed me a skullcap. It sat precariously on my head. He draped a prayer shawl over my shoulders. It sent up a cloud of dust that danced in a shaft of sunlight trickling through the window. He gave me a black-bound prayer book. I told him I could not read it.

He shook his head. "A stickler, we got. I ask if you're a Jew, you tell me you don't believe. I hand you a book, you tell me you can't read. Who said anything about reading? Stand up and be counted is all you got to do."

The eight other men drew closer. I took a step back. He reached out a freckle-spattered hand and reeled me in again. They began to pray. It was no different from last time. I did not understand the words. I did not respond to the rhythm. All around me, men bent their knees and pitched their bodies forward, bent and pitched, but I stood straight-kneed and stiff-necked. Once, though, toward the end, my knees buckled for a moment, and in that fragment of memory, I was back in the Synagogengemeinde Osnabrück, standing beside my father, toying with the fringe of his prayer shawl, the one I would grow into when I was thirteen, only I never had. By the time I was thirteen, we had left Osnabrück for Amsterdam. By the time I was thirteen, no one could afford to be a Jew.

A chorus of amens rose to the ceiling like a flock of birds flushed out of a swamp. They would have made easy targets. I took off the prayer shawl and skullcap, put them on one of the wooden benches, and started up the aisle, but the redhead was too fast for me.

"What took you so long?" he asked, as he trotted along beside me.

I did not answer.

"A lot of mornings between, we could have used you. We don't have a minyan, we can't pray."

I stopped and turned to him. "Why?"

"What do you mean, why? Ten men make a minyan. You need a minyan to pray. It's the law."

"But why is it the law? Who made it up? Who wrote it down? I know about the Constitution and the founding fathers. I know how state and federal laws are made. But what authority says you need ten men to pray? Don't tell me God."

"Again with the God and the belief."

"All I want to know is who says nine believers aren't better than nine believers and one apostate like me?"

"Apostate?"

"Lapsed."

"I know what the word means. Pretty fancy. Like a big cathedral, with stained-glass windows."

"Or why not one? What if I want to come here and pray alone?"

"You won't even pray with us. You want to pray alone?"

"What if I did?"

"Be my guest."

"You mean I wouldn't need nine other men?"

"Only for certain prayers."

"But why? That's what I want to know."

"You understood Hebrew, you'd know. In Hebrew, you don't pray *I*, you pray *we*."

"So?"

"So, you pray we, it means you're not alone. It means you got a responsibility to other people. It means, in answer to Cain's question, yeah, you are."

"My brother's keeper?"

"Brother, father, son, second cousin twice removed, the schmo next door who isn't even in the family."

"What if they're all dead?"

"Dead, living, what's the difference? You still got obligations."

"That's why you come here?"

He shrugged and smiled. "You got a better reason?"

He went on grinning up at me. His two front teeth—the work of a DP camp dentist, I was willing to bet—beamed like blinding white beacons in a mouth full of yellow. The wild red hair glinted like a burning bush. What in hell was I doing here? The man came because he had no place else to go. He came because he was afraid not to come. But I lived in another world. I was not afraid. Only these days I was.

"So, what's eating you, Mr. Smarty Pants who knows all about the founding fathers, and I'm not talking Abraham, Isaac, and Jacob. Besides, you're walking around in goyish shoes."

"How did you know?"

"Last time you came, I watched you leave. You got Jersey plates on your car. You don't cross state lines to go to shul unless you're hiding something. The way I figure it, the hiding gets too much, you come here."

"I'm not hiding. I made a choice. I built a new life."

"Mazel tov. So, I repeat, what're you doing here?"

The sun shot through his wild red hair. I had to blink against the light.

"Have you ever heard of Anne Frank?"

"You know someone who hasn't?"

"I'm Peter van Pels. Van Daan in the diary."

I waited for the sneer of disbelief. Every few years someone claimed to be Princess Anastasia. There were still women who insisted they saw Rudolph Valentino. Houdinis were a dime a dozen.

"So?"

"You believe me?"

"What's not to believe? The world's full of Nazis who never were. Why shouldn't a few Jews go missing?"

"Not everybody sees it that way."

"You've been taking a poll?"

"The whole world thinks I'm dead, and Pfeffer's a fool, and my father's a thief."

"Now you lost me."

"In the play and the movie."

"A big theatergoer, I'm not."

"My father never stole bread. But in the play and the movie they have him stealing bread. You know why? So the audience won't get bored. The Green Police breathing down our necks; the good Dutch citizens ready to turn us in for seven-fifty florins a head, and rising; the Nazi bastards, who don't even care about the money, who do it for the fun, aren't enough to keep them on the edge of their seats. They need a father taking bread out of his son's mouth. They need my father taking bread out of my mouth."

"So?"

"So it's driving me crazy that I can't do anything about it."

He shook his head. The burning bush trembled in the sour air. "So now you understand about the minyan."

■   ■   ■   ■

I RENTED a box in the post office in the next town. I did not want acquaintances to see me getting mail away from my home or office. George Johnson would think I had something on the side, either romantic or financial. Harry would wonder what was up. The man behind the counter in the post office took my money and gave me a key and a slip of paper with a string of digits on it. I was a number again.

That evening I closed the door to my office and sat at my desk to write the letter.

Mr. Otto Frank

Herbstgasse 11

Basel, Switzerland.

I was not interested in reparations or royalties or recognition, I explained. Especially not recognition. All I wanted was the truth, as both he and I knew it. He was famous. When he spoke, people paid attention. He had even founded the Anne Frank Stichting. Now she was an institute, as well as a legend and a saint. My hand flew over the page. Justice, I wrote, and decency; conscience and honor; a man's reputation, a man's life. I demanded action. Looking back at it now, I do not know what I expected Otto to do. Hire men to walk back and forth in front of theaters with sandwich boards saying do not mistake this movie for the real thing? Take out ads in the paper proclaiming Hermann van Pels is not a thief? There was a man suing Otto who actually had taken out an ad in the newspaper. I had seen it and read about the lawsuit. It was a nasty business, and I had no intention of getting mixed up in that. But there were other methods. A public statement from Otto. A disclaimer before the movie. A paragraph in playbills around the world. I finished the letter, dropped it in the mailbox in front of the local post office, and drove home with one hand on the wheel.

I did not expect to hear from Otto for some time, but that did not stop me from going to the post office in the neighboring town daily to look for his reply. Each evening I stopped on my way home, took out the key, unlocked the small glass door with the number on the front, swung it open, and peered inside. Night after night, I gazed into a small empty cell. A week went by, then a second, and a third. On the day the next month's rent for the box was due, I swung open the small glass door, bent, and peered inside. An envelope was leaning against one side of the box. I drew it out. The stock was stiff and heavy in my hand. I stood staring down at the address. *Mr. Peter van Pels* sat on top of the post office box number. A series of names, like a small legal army, marched across the upper left-hand corner of the envelope.

I pried open the flap. Inside was a single piece of paper of the same creamy stock. I unfolded it. Again my name sat above the number. My eye raced down the page. The writer, who represented Mr. Otto Frank, wished to inform me that official Red Cross records of survivors listed no Peter van Pels. The last Mr. Frank had seen of the Peter van Pels who had been in hiding with him at 263 Prinsengracht was in the hospital at Auschwitz. The memory was extremely painful to Mr. Frank. He had pleaded with the boy to stay. The boy had said he would take his chances on the forced march. Mr. Frank still blamed himself for failing to persuade the boy, who had been like a son to him.

There was one more paragraph. Any further attempt to harass Mr. Otto Frank or impersonate anyone connected with the story of Anne Frank would be met with legal action.

I sat on the worn wooden bench in the center of the room and read the letter through again. I had not expected the red-haired man in the synagogue to believe me. I knew strangers would be skeptical. But Otto knew me. For two years and twenty-three days, we had lived together in rank, suffocating proximity. In the camp, I had taken him food, and as the letter said, he had tried to persuade me to stay behind with him in the hospital. He had told me I was like a son to him. And now he did not believe in my existence.

I MADE one more attempt. I wrote to my uncle, the one who had sent the money to me in the DP camp. He knew I had survived the war. He would vouch for who I was. He would help me right the wrongs Otto had committed.

His reply arrived in less than a week, but then, unlike Otto, he did not have to turn the matter over to attorneys. *To whom it may concern,* it said. Not *Dear Peter,* not even *Mr. van Pels.* Whoever I was, and my name might, in fact, be Peter van Pels, I was not the child he remembered, the son of the brother he loved. That Peter van Pels would not have bilked him of money to come to this country, then disappeared. That Peter van Pels had some family feeling.

"If Anne Frank could return from among the murdered, she would be appalled at the misuse to which her journal entries had been put."
—"The Uses—and Misuses—of a Young Girl's Diary," by Lawrence L. Langer, in *Anne Frank: Reflections on Her Life and Legacy*, edited by Hyman A. Enzer and Sandra Solotoroff-Enzer

"'The Diary of Anne Frank,' the Pulitzer Prize-winning Broadway success, has run into an involved breach of contract law fight in Supreme Court. . . . Mr. Levin charged his adaptation was discriminated against as 'too Jewish.' . . . Mr. Bloomgarden . . . called the 'Jewishness' argument absurd and wholly false."
—*New York World-Telegram and Sun*, March 18, 1957

"If you really love me, you will take a gun and shoot Otto Frank."
—Meyer Levin to his wife, quoted in *The Hidden Life of Otto Frank*, by Carol Ann Lee

SEVENTEEN

■ ■ I DID NOT WANT TO get mixed up in the lawsuit against
■ ■ Otto. But my father demanded exoneration. My children begged to be hugged, and tucked in, and taken for drives. I had to do something. I wrote a third letter. This one was to a man named Meyer Levin. Levin had written a play based on Anne's diary. He had undertaken the project, he said, at the

urging of Otto Frank. His version was, he claimed, faithful to her intent. He spoke, he insisted, in the true voice of Anne Frank. I did not understand how a middle-aged American writer, whose only experience of the camps was as a correspondent attached to the U.S. Ninth Air Force when it liberated Buchenwald, came to believe he spoke in the voice of a typhoid-ridden girl whose breath had expired in Bergen-Belsen, but that was beside the point. Levin swore the play that ran on Broadway and around the world was a pack of lies. He was a man after my own heart.

Levin wrote back immediately. I read his reply on the same wooden bench in the post office where I had read the letters from Otto's attorneys and my uncle telling me that I did not exist. Levin had no doubts about my identity. At least, he did not express any in his letter. He wanted to know how soon we could meet. He was eager to show me a dossier that indicated Otto Frank had survived Auschwitz only because of his communist connections, and, as proof, detailed Otto's travels through Soviet territory on his way from the camp back to Amsterdam. He accused Otto of killing his play, as the Nazis had killed Anne, and for the same reason. His play beat with a Jewish heart and burned with a Jewish soul, and Otto was a communist-sympathizing anti-Semite and a self-hating Jew. He included his telephone number and asked me to call him immediately. He spoke of a book telling my side of the story, and after that, a play recounting the true tale of Anne Frank, and of me, Peter van Daan—the typed *van Daan* was crossed out and *van Pels* was scrawled in pencil above it—the boy who had loved her. In closing, he urged me not to waste another minute. The world was waiting for my story. I owed it to Anne. I owed it to history. I owed it to him, a voice for Jewry, a truth-teller, an artist. He also cautioned me not to communicate with anyone else about this momentous matter until we met and executed the necessary contracts. There were many issues regarding publication, publicity, and subsidiary rights, which a nonprofessional like me could not be expected to anticipate or understand. He was not speaking only of the financial arrangements. Though he was not a rich man, his current novel, *Compulsion,* was doing extremely well. To put it bluntly, he was not in this for the money. As proof of that, he had promised to turn every penny he was awarded in his suit, above legal expenses, over to Jewish charities. He cared only about the memory of Anne Frank and six million others. All he wanted was that her true voice be heard. He was certain I felt the same. He looked forward to meeting me, wished me all good health, and signed himself, most sincerely, Meyer Levin.

There was a postscript. He asked if I had a family, perhaps a daughter, and wanted to know if she was old enough for television appearances.

I tore the letter into pieces, threw them in the large trash can overflowing with unsolicited flyers and unwanted advertisements, and went to the desk at the front of the post office. I handed the clerk the key to the box. He said my rental had another eighteen days to run and warned that he could not give me back my money. I told him I did not expect a refund. He asked if I wanted to leave a forwarding address. I told him I had no forwarding address. I added there was no place I could be reached. I mentioned, on my way out, that I was leaving the country for an extended period of time.

■　■　■　■

A FEW weeks later, I was heading north on the New Jersey Turnpike toward lower Manhattan. I would not get mixed up in Meyer Levin's misguided schemes, but I did want to witness the trial. When he exposed the play as a pack of lies, I would be there to hear my father exonerated in an American court of law.

Many people were scandalized at the very idea of the trial. What kind of man would sue the father of a saint? The Jewish community was especially up in arms. The Jewish community is one of my father-in-law's favorite expressions, as if we, or rather they, are one big happy family; no capos; no black marketeers; no shadowy figures stealing through the gray zone of survival; no, in this case, grown men fighting over the body of a dead child. Some pillars of this so-called community championed Levin's cause. Others demanded that poor Otto be left in peace. A third contingent raised their voices in a chorus of shushes. Don't wash dirty linen in public. Don't air differences before the goyim. Surely two well-intentioned men could find common ground. But they could not. The trial opened in the New York State Supreme Court in lower Manhattan on a Friday morning in mid-December.

Otto was the first person I saw as I entered the courthouse, and the second, and fifth. That was the back of Otto's head stepping into an elevator, and his profile in conversation with another man, and his walk preceding me down the corridor. Then I did see him. I stopped and squinted down the hall. I could not believe it, though he was the reason I was here.

He was coming toward me, walking slowly, his hand cupping the elbow of a woman at his side, his new wife, I guessed, his head bent, his back still straight. Another man, this one in an expensive-looking cashmere coat, walked on his other side, whispering in his ear as they went. I stopped and waited. My heart was thumping so wildly I was sure it was visible beneath my shirt and suit jacket and overcoat. He was getting closer now. I willed him to look up. He lifted his gaze from the scuffed marble floor. I held my breath. His eyes went through me. I might as well not have existed.

I felt my mouth forming his name, but I could not spit it out. He kept going past me. I watched his German-army-stiffened back as he went. Turn around, I dared him. Turn around, you lying son-of-a-bitch. But I did not speak, and Otto did not turn.

What had I expected? The last time he saw me, I was a boy, wasted from hunger, covered with scabs and lice, hunch-shouldered with fear. The lawyer's letter was right. That Peter van Pels had died at the end of the war. I turned, followed Otto down the corridor, and moved with the rest of the spectators into the courtroom.

The judge's bench, flanked by state and national flags, loomed at the far end. Alexander Hamilton and Dwight D. Eisenhower and Averell Harriman looked down sternly from their gilt frames. The room reeked of seriousness and probity. I found the atmosphere encouraging.

I took a seat in the back, slipped out of my overcoat, and folded it on my lap, but just as I settled in, the judge entered, and we all stood. I do not usually like pomp, but in this case I found it reassuring. We sat and I arranged my bulky coat again. If it had not been a court of law, I would have taken off my jacket as well. The room was solemn, but overheated.

While the judge and the lawyers went through the preliminaries, I studied the twelve men in the jury box. They looked self-conscious and stunned to be there. None of them gave an appearance of particular mental prowess. That was all right too. The American legal system was built on a jury of peers. How smart did they have to be to tell true from false? My ten-year-old daughter did it on papers dotted with gold stars all the time.

Levin was sitting at one of the two tables in the front of the courtroom. I recognized him from photographs and television appearances. He was bull-necked and broad-shouldered, with a wide face shadowed by heavy eyebrows. His hair rose from a receding hairline in tight coils, as if ready to spring. When the attorney called him to the stand, he crossed the courtroom on the balls of his feet, like a boxer.

The attorney began by questioning his early dealings with Otto Frank. He had no written contract to adapt the diary, Levin admitted, but he did have an understanding. "I trusted Mr. Frank."

The man in front of me was leaning forward in his seat. Beside him, an older man, a refugee, don't ask me how I knew, I just did, cupped a hand behind his ear to catch Levin's words. My eye continued down the row. It stopped at the woman in the last seat. I had assumed she was still in Amsterdam, or perhaps back in Germany. She was not Jewish. She had nothing to fear. But it could not be anyone else. I was sure of it, I thought.

I leaned forward to get a better look at her profile. Her chin had settled into a small rounded pouch. A line, dark as a crayon mark, hung from her mouth like an unhappy comma. Beneath a dispirited brown hat, her blond curls were a tarnished-silver yellow. Her suit was brown too, with a moth-eaten fur collar. I had not seen anything like it since I had left the Marseilles. The suit made me think she was not living in America, only visiting. She had come for the trial. She had come for her husband, though, as my mother used to point out to my father, if not to Pfeffer, he was not really her husband. My father always shushed my mother when she said that. Only the racial laws had prevented Pfeffer from marrying Charlotte. You could not blame Lotte for that, he insisted. My father always did have a soft spot for Charlotte. Who could blame him? She was a Jean Harlow type. She must have been in her thirties the few times I met her before we disappeared, but at night between sour-smelling sheets—even when we could get soap after we went into hiding, it was no match for the filth in our lives—the years between Charlotte Pfeffer and me fell away. Sitting in a New York State courtroom, under the stern gaze of Alexander Hamilton and Dwight D. Eisenhower and Averell Harriman, I heard the echo of my own stifled groans as I lie on the cot under the stairs and couple with the memory of Charlotte I had taken into hiding with me. Then my father's shouting drowns out the sound.

"We tiptoe around in our stocking feet all day, we can't even take a pee for fear someone will hear, and Romeo here is sending love letters through Miep. Why don't you just hang a flag out the window? *Jews in hiding.*"

Pfeffer's voice, tight with wounded dignity, pitiful with suppressed tears, comes back at him. "It's easy for you to talk, you and Frank, with your wives and children. I have not seen my wife in more than a year. Who knows where my son is? Somewhere in England was the last I heard."

Lucky him, I used to think, lucky Werner Pfeffer somewhere in England. Fortunate boy whose father had the foresight to get him on a kindertransport in the nick of time.

I sat watching Charlotte as I listened to Meyer Levin's testimony. He talked of misrepresentation. He used the word deceit. He spoke of disrespect. Charlotte's age-slackened chin went up and down in agreement.

When I arrived in the courtroom the following Monday morning, she was sitting in the same place she had occupied the previous Friday. There was an empty seat beside her. I could not resist. I wanted to get a better look at her. I was curious if she would recognize anything in me. It seemed unlikely. Otto, who had lived with me during those years, had not known me. Charlotte had met me only a few times, when I was still a boy.

I stopped at the end of the row where she was sitting and asked if the place next to her was taken. She looked up. I waited. She said it was not. I murmured excuse me, as I slid past her and took the seat at her side.

On Tuesday we returned to the same places and exchanged good mornings. By Wednesday I was helping her off and on with her coat. It was as shabby as the suit she had worn the first day. She had moved the moth-eaten fur collar to it. When the court recessed for lunch on Thursday, I asked if she would care to join me. She hesitated, then smiled. It was the smile of a woman who has forgotten for a moment that she is an old lady, and I was glad. The smile meant my memories of her were not lies.

She said she would like to very much, held out her hand in its mended glove, and introduced herself as Mrs. Pfeffer. I told her my name was Harry Wolfe. "Like the animal," I added, "but with an *e*."

We came out of the courthouse into the winter light and made our way through crowds of purposefully moving people, carrying bright bulging shopping bags. Christmas was only six days away. Pedestrians came between us, and I had to take

Charlotte's elbow to stay together. At one point, she stopped in front of a window with a larger-than-life Santa Claus.

"When my husband was alive, we celebrated Chanukah as well as Christmas." She looked from the window to me. "Do you know what Chanukah is, Mr. Wolfe?" I told her I did. "That is something else I cannot forgive. They make him ignorant of his religion. The man was a master of the Hebrew language, and they turn him into a child who does not know about his own holiday."

"Pardon me?" I said, but she only shook her head and turned away from the window. We started walking again.

Inside the restaurant, I managed to get us a booth. It was not quiet, but it was not as noisy as the tables in the middle of the room. Shouted orders and rattled dishes and the echo of several dozen conversations rained down from the high tin ceiling. I apologized for the noise and explained that at this hour, in this neighborhood, lunch was bound to be hectic.

"Americans are always in a hurry," she said.

"You're not an American?"

"I live in Amsterdam. I am here only a few weeks. As long as the trial continues."

The waiter appeared, pencil and pad in hand, but Charlotte spoke to me when she ordered, and I passed the message on to him.

"You came all this distance just for the trial?" I asked when the waiter left.

"You have seen the play they speak of in the trial? The cause of all the trouble?" I nodded. "You know the character of the dentist?"

"Dussel," I said, though it was a cruel thing to do.

"Dussel was not his name. The child made that up." She shook her head. The curls trembled beneath her cheerless hat. "That is one more thing I cannot forgive. A young girl calls a man a dussel, and it means nothing. A book calls a man a fool, and he is labeled for all to see. A child writes in her diary that a man, a fine man she should respect, has a screw loose, and it is impertinent. A man publishes this impertinence for the world to believe as truth, and it is a humiliation. My husband said she was a sweet child, and clever, but undisciplined. I make no judgments. It could not have been easy, a young girl and a grown man, a man who is missing his own family, sharing a tiny room."

I told her I did not understand.

"The man in the play, the dentist who shares the room with Anne Frank, his name was not Dussel but Pfeffer. Fritz Pfeffer. I am his widow."

"The play does not mention that he was married," I said, though that was cruel too.

"We were husband and wife." The soft chin grew sturdy. "The racial laws of the Nazis prevented Jews and gentiles from marrying, but we were husband and wife all the same. After the war, the Dutch government recognized the marriage. I have the certificate."

You see, Mammichen, he made an honest woman of her after all, or the Dutch government did.

"That is one of the many things the play lies about. It shows my dear husband as a man without family, but he had a wife, and a son from his first marriage. He was raising the boy himself, but immediate after Kristallnacht, he saw the danger and had the distant sight to send Werner on a kindertransport. It is not easy, to send away a child you love. It grieved him. But England, he knew, will be better for the boy. There will be the bombs, but there will not be the Nazis. So he sent Werner away."

Lucky Werner, I thought again, and was surprised that the envy could remain so long after the danger had passed. I remembered running into him in the customs shed the day I arrived in America. He was looking for someone who had known his father. He was in the market for memories. I had pretended I knew no one by the name of Pfeffer. I was protecting myself, but I was also sparing him. The last he had seen of his father, Pfeffer was standing on a station platform waving goodbye to a train full of children headed west to safety. I saw Pfeffer packed into a cattle car going east to Auschwitz. He remembered strong arms lifting him out of a skiff. On the back of the photo Pfeffer had kept in his room were the words *Werner's first boat trip, Whit-Sunday, 1932.* I saw that same arm, bruised and bleeding from the careless but not unintentional swing of a guard's rifle butt, as Pfeffer held it out to be tattooed. Leave well enough alone, I should have told Werner in the customs shed. Don't go looking for memories you will not be able to forget.

"His son has not come with you for the trial?" I asked.

She frowned and shook her head. "It would have been easier for him than for me. Werner is here in America. California. But he is no longer Werner Pfeffer. Now he calls himself Peter Pepper. He is a grown man and can do as he likes, but I cannot pretend happiness. He should have stayed Pfeffer. He owes that much to his father."

I agreed with her. I had not changed my name, though I owed less. Of course, I had not had to. A good American name, the customs officer had said.

"Let sleeping dogs lie, Werner tells me."

So Werner, now Peter, like me, has learned, after all.

"But I cannot. That is why I write to Mr. Frank. We are old friends. My husband and I know Mr. Frank and his wife before the war even. After, too, he is kind to me. Many Saturday nights, we come together with Miep and Jan, the people who help them in the hiding, to play cards. Before my husband's pension begins, Mr. Frank is generous to lend me money. So when he wants to publish his daughter's diary, I say nothing. If he finds comfort in putting out the child's words for the world to read, it is not for me to forbid. But the play is another matter. I tell him I will not stand for the play. I tell him I will sue. Do you know what he says?"

She put down her fork and leaned toward me across the table. Every emotion had a physical manifestation. She shrugged her shoulders, and tossed her head, and could not help reaching out to lay on hands. Perhaps that, as much as the Jean Harlow looks, was what had drawn both my father and me.

"That I should not be so childish to think these powerful people do not know from the legal point of view what they are allowed to write."

Oh, Otto, that was not worthy of you. And to think you accused me of having no strength of character.

"He is trying to frighten me. But he does not understand I have nothing left to fear. I have already lost my dear husband. All I have left is his memory. That I must fight for. So I write to the people who made the play, this Mr. and Mrs. Hackett." She shrugged her shoulders and shook her head again, as if warning me not to expect too much. "First they do not answer. I think they are afraid. They know this is not right. They know even a poor widow can sue, no matter what Otto Frank says about the legal point of view. Finally I receive a letter. It is worse than Otto's. It is crazy. They say that they must portray my Fritz as a buffoon so that the world will not forget the terrible things that happen. They say if people do not have a dussel to laugh at, they will not come to see the play, and they will not hear this important message these Hacketts have to tell. This I do not understand. Millions of people dead, and no one will grieve for them unless they make a fool of my Fritz?" The words had pushed her forward across the table. Now she sat back in her chair. "Forgive me, Mr. Wolfe. I am too excitable. But it is not just. That Otto Frank should be a hero in the world, and my dear Fritz a laughingstock. That is why I have come. To hear Otto Frank admit the truth."

I sat looking across the table at her. Today she was wearing the threadbare blue suit that she alternated with the shabby brown. I wondered where she had found the money to make the trip. Not from Pfeffer's pension, I was willing to bet. Had she borrowed from friends? Had she pawned possessions? She wore no jewelry other than a plain gold wedding band.

"You came all this way just for that?"

She straightened her shoulders and lifted her chin. "You think that is not enough? You think to hear the truth said aloud, to see my dear husband's name cleared, his memory restored, his fineness respected, is so little?" She leaned toward me across the table again. Her eyes singed my face. "Tell me, Mr. Wolfe, if it is someone you loved, if it is your father rather than my husband, you would not come halfway around the world, you would not move heaven and earth to right the wrong?"

I bumped the table as I stood. The water in the glasses

sloshed back and forth. "We ought to hurry," I said. "We don't want to miss the afternoon session."

EVERY FEW days I came up with a new piece of property, some distance away, that I had to visit. That was my excuse for being out of the office.

"You sure you're okay, pal?" Harry asked one evening when I telephoned him.

"I'm fine," I told him, "but if you want to look it over, go ahead. If you don't trust my judgment—"

He did not let me finish. I knew he would not. Nonetheless, I was beginning to wonder how long the trial would last. It was the end of the second week, and no one had yet broached the real issues. Charlotte and I sat, shoulder to shoulder, waiting for Meyer Levin, the man who spoke in the true voice of Anne Frank, to point out that Fritz Pfeffer had not been a fool, and my father had not been a thief. The longer the lies were allowed to stand, the more I began to doubt my memory. If I remembered my father with a mustache and my mother not at all, perhaps I had got this wrong too, despite my rereading of the diary. Maybe Anne had left my father's theft out of her diary, but Otto had recalled it for the playwrights. I brought the subject up at lunch with Charlotte.

"I was wondering," I began, "if the play maligns your husband, perhaps it's unfair to some of the others too."

She nodded and laid crimson fingertips on my arm. "You are a very clever young man, Mr. Wolfe. The play is a travesty. The movie too. You know the mother, not Mrs. Frank, the other one, Mrs. van Pels, the one they call Mrs. van Daan?"

I nodded.

"She was a lovely woman. And generous. On the birthday of Miep, the girl in Mr. Frank's office who helped hide them, Mrs. van Pels presented her with an onyx and diamond ring. Miep did not want to take it. Already she has sold Mrs. van Pels's fur coat for them, and she knows the money and the things to sell are running out. But Mrs. van Pels insists. She says she and her husband want to give Miep something to show their gratitude."

I had forgotten the ring. I saw my parents going through the few pieces of jewelry my mother had left. This was not good enough. That was too good and would feed us for several weeks. Finally, they settled on the ring my father had given my mother for an anniversary several years earlier. My mother had been reluctant to part with it because of the sentimental value, but my father had said that would make it even more valuable to Miep.

"What about the husband? Mr. van Daan."

"You mean Mr. van Pels. A charming gentleman." She glanced beyond me, as if the past were right over my shoulder, and her mouth curled into a wistful crescent. So she had known my father liked her. Her eyes came back to me. "Never have I seen such a cultivated nose." She tapped the side of her own with her index finger. "There was not a spice he could not identify. A single whiff of a sausage, of any dish, and he could tell you. Paprika, thyme, rosemary, cardamom. It does not matter how many spices or how exotic. Mr. van Pels knows. He was very sensitive. Nothing like the boorish man in the play."

I had forgotten his nose too. Was there anything I remembered?

"And yet, sensitive as he was, with his cultivated nose, he stole bread out of the others' mouths."

She shook her head. "Impossible."

"Are you saying that isn't true either."

"It is made up, just as they make up the things about my husband."

"How can you be sure? You weren't there."

"I knew Mr. van Pels. He would not do such a thing. If he did, my husband would write me about it. This is one more truth that the trial must tell."

But though the testimony dragged on, no one so much as mentioned the names of my father and Charlotte's husband, not even the made up names. An American rabbi, who had spent the war in a synagogue not far from Hollywood, complained that the play, which Otto had permitted to be made from his daughter's diary, was not sufficiently Jewish. A scholar testified that, according to mathematical calculations, less than twenty percent of Anne's diary had anything to do with Jewish matters. Charges and countercharges flew across the overheated courtroom. Bitterness sizzled in the hot air. Grown men raised their voices to stuff words they wanted to hear in a dead girl's mouth. But they got no nearer the truth. When they reached the summations, I knew I had to act. I was not going to make a scene. I simply wanted to set the record straight. I wanted to explain that Anne was a child. Sometimes she believed, sometimes she doubted. One day she thought people were good, the next she hated everyone, including her parents and sister, especially, locked in that stinking annex, her parents and sister. She was a growing girl, writing her thoughts down in a red-plaid diary she had got for her birthday, until the space ran out, and she scribbled on any scrap of paper she could get her hands on. And I wanted to tell them about my father, who

had not stolen bread, but had taken chances to make arrangements before we went into hiding, so the butcher would give
Miep meat, no rations required, no questions asked, and all of
us in the annex would eat. I wanted to explain that my mother
was not a shameless embarrassing flirt, but a high-spirited
huge-hearted woman, who baked babkas laced with love and
gave away jewelry fraught with value. I wanted to tell them to
stop bickering about what Anne believed, which signified
nothing more than the growing pains of a young girl, and pay
attention to what my parents had done, which shouted the
truth of who they were.

I stood. I was staring straight ahead at the judge, but I felt
faces turning toward me. Attention spread like ripples around
the pebble of truth I was about to fling.

"Your Honor," I began. You see, I was not disrespectful.

The judge's gavel came down. The word *order* soared above
my head.

"Your Honor," I repeated, "I would just like—"

Every head in the courtroom turned to me. People craned
their necks to see who was making the disturbance. Only it was
not a disturbance. If the judge would just stop banging his
gavel, I would make my statement, quietly, reasonably, respect-
fully, and sit down.

"Your Honor," I shouted, because by now I had no choice
but to raise my voice.

Out of the corner of my eye, I saw the guards closing in,
two moving up the aisle from the front of the courtroom, two
down from the back. I did not have much time.

"I have a statement," I began. At my side, I felt Charlotte
shrinking away. I tried to hold on to her. We would make a

united front. We would clear her husband and my father in a single stroke. But one of the guards shouldered between us. A second grabbed me from the row behind.

"You don't understand," I called to the judge.

The guards were dragging me out of the row of seats.

"I am Peter van Pels," I insisted, as they hustled me up the aisle. "She is Charlotte Pfeffer, and I am Peter van Pels." I was hanging on to the last row of seats now. I would not let them throw me out of the courtroom. I would be heard.

"Tell them, Charlotte," I pleaded, but Charlotte was shaking her head and trying to get as far from me as possible.

"Tell them, Otto!" But Otto had disappeared from view within the protective circle of his defense attorneys.

The guards pried my hands free. "Tell them the truth about my father," I begged, as they strong-armed me through the doors.

One of the guards had a hammerlock around my neck. "I am Peter van Pels." His hold was like iron. I flailed backward at his face.

Another guard closed in. He was trying to pin my arms to my side. I pulled my right arm free. "I am Peter van Pels," I warned him, as my fist moved toward his jaw. I felt something hard and solid in my stomach. "I am Peter van Pels," I confided to the marble floor, as it came up to meet me.

"Who the hell is Peter van Pels?" I heard the guard ask just before my head hit the hard surface.

"He was beaten by the SS and said that he had promised himself he would avenge the death of his relatives and his own sufferings. . . . He knew where one German lived by himself. He stealthily approached him and beat him with his fists, but he still felt unavenged. He found a nearby axe and described in detail how he killed the man with the axe in cold blood with his own hands. He said after he saw the lacerated corpse he felt better and went home. . . . At no time [since] has his behavior indicated any of the murderous traits indicated."

—A psychiatric report from
Camp Fohrenwald, Team 106

EIGHTEEN

■ ■ I WAS BACK IN DR. GABOR'S OFFICE. This time there
■ ■ was no reason. I had not lost my voice. My vision was twenty-twenty. My only symptom was an outburst of honesty. Truth-telling landed me in a psychiatrist's office. I know that is what patients always say, but in this case it was accurate.

When Madeleine had come to get me after the incident in the courtroom, the police told her I had disrupted the proceedings by insisting I was Peter van Pels. She got huffy then, my good little wife.

"What's wrong with that? He is Peter van Pels."

"Doesn't mean he's got to yell about it in a New York State courtroom, ma'am."

In the car on the way home, she said I had to go back to Dr. Gabor. Gabor or someone like him.

"Ah, but there's no one quite like our Dr. Gabor," I said. I wanted to show her I had not lost my sense of humor.

She started to cry. "If you refuse to get help, Peter, I'll take the children and leave. I swear to God, this time I mean it."

I believed her. The memory of the boy she'd mistaken me for had atrophied. The expectations she'd had of me had withered. I told her I would make an appointment the first thing in the morning. I did not even argue that it was a waste of perfectly good money. There was nothing wrong with me anymore. It was Otto, and that crazy writer who thought he spoke in Anne's voice, and the rest of the world that was sick. But I was too exhausted to argue. My muscles ached. That was from the skirmish with the court guards. My nerves twitched. My mind was sore. It would be so easy to give up. I felt the words rising in my chest. There's something I have to tell you . . . about the years in Amsterdam . . . about Auschwitz . . . about my circumcised penis. The innocence would drain from the eyes she was determined not to close. A cataract of fear would cloud her vision. I remembered the shame I had seen on Abigail's face when I caught her staring at my number. I clamped my mouth shut. I had acted irresponsibly in court, but I had not lost all sense of decency.

UNLIKE MY red-haired friend, Gabor needed to refresh his memory about who I was. He sat studying a folder full of papers while I waited across the desk from him. It was still cluttered with the tools of his trade, and primitive symbols, and those sad martyrs from Calais. Nothing in the office had changed, except the doctor. He looked more prosperous than ever, but that might have been the deep polished-mahogany tinge to his face and hands.

"Been south?" I asked while he browsed through the notes he had written about me years before.

"Mmm," was all he answered.

He closed the folder, leaned back in his chair, fixed me across the desk with that inane owl's stare, and asked what brought me back.

I had made up my mind. This time I would tell him the truth. He was not someone I had to protect. I would tell him everything, or almost everything. There was one matter I could not afford to confess. I was an American citizen, a pillar of the community, but that did not mean I could not be deported or extradited.

I began with the boy in the diary.

"You believe me?" I asked when he had written it all down.

"Why not?"

"Otto Frank didn't. At least he pretended not to." I told him about my letter to Otto and the answer from his attorneys.

"Maybe he's not pretending. After the war, when your name wasn't on the list of survivors, he concluded you were dead. He's been living with that sorrow for a long time. It might be too painful for him to entertain hope."

"If he's so heartbroken, why did he denigrate my father's memory? He's afraid to believe I'm alive."

"Are you so clear about how and when everything hap-pened?"

I thought of my mother's blond hair and my father's mustache. "I remember the important things."

He looked down at the file he had left open on his desk. "Your father died in Auschwitz, correct?"

"We've been through this."

"In the selection, that first night on the train platform?"

I nodded.

He rifled through the pages in the folder. They were covered with scrawls. His handwriting was as muddled as his office.

"Unless he died a few months later, when you watched him being marched off with a group of other men, then saw the clothes in the truck when it came back."

I could not recall telling him either account, though I remembered both of them.

"I'm not trying to catch you out, Mr. van Pels. Both deaths are real in your head."

In my head. I could have murdered him for that.

"My father's dead, and you tell me it doesn't matter how I killed him."

"How you killed him?"

"How they killed him."

He stared across the desk at me with that idiotic gaze.

"I am not a murderer."

"I never suggested you were."

"That night in the barn was an aberration."

He waited.

"It was right after the war. We were still hungry, for Christ's sake. That's how soon after the war it was."

He went on staring at me.

"We just wanted to have some fun. And get a little of our own back."

"Your own?"

"Revenge. Hell, we deserved it, after what we'd been through. He deserved what he got too. The war's over, and all of a sudden he's just an innocent farmer. Like he never heard of the SS Like he didn't have the fucking tattoo to prove it. The tattoo and those mean little eyes and that pig's snout of a nose."

"You had some sort of run-in with an SS man?"

"The bastard only got what was coming to him."

"Tell me about it," he said.

I had thought he would never ask.

The others had had enough. Come on, they said. We've had our fun. We hurt some Germans. We made some money. But I could not stop. The hunger still gnawed. I had beaten up a few men. I had broken some windows, taken a pair of boots and a bottle of schnapps, stolen some money. Penny-ante stuff. Crumbs of revenge. I craved a banquet. And I knew where to find it. Everyone knew about the farmer, what he had done during the war, what he was just waiting to start doing again.

The unpainted wood glinted in moonlight thin as water. The door to the barn was open. The son-of-a-bitch was a lousy farmer, on top of everything else.

The stench of animals and manure and sweat and piss and alcohol made me gasp. The only stink missing was fear. The farmer was unconscious. I was fearless.

Rats scuttled in the darkness. I took another step inside. An animal snorted. Something pawed the ground. Snores sawed the sickening air. Shapes began to take form in the darkness. I made out a haunch, a snout, a heap of filthy clothing, an axe. The clothing went up and down in rhythm with the snoring. The shaft of the axe fit my hand as if it had been made for it.

I used both hands to lift the axe, but it fell of its own weight. Blood spurted into the watery moonlight. I raise the axe again, and it falls a second time, a third, until I stop counting. Blood makes a black puddle on the hard dirt floor. Moonlight flickers in the pool like a flame. I drop the axe on top of the heap of stinking clothing. My stolen boots skid through the blood as I begin to run.

When I finished the story, I took out my handkerchief and mopped my face. The sweat was pouring out of me as if I were still hacking away with that axe. Gabor was lolling back in his chair, cool as a cucumber.

"So you went to the barn and you killed the SS bastard with an axe. Good for you. If you really did."

"What do you mean, if I really did? I just told you I did. I never told anyone else in my life."

"You never told anyone? Not the others you were with that night?"

"I told you, they had had enough. They left."

"What about in the DP camp? Perhaps you mentioned it during the psychological evaluation?"

"Are you crazy? You think I would have got into this country if I had told them that?"

"So no one could have stolen your story?"

"What do you mean, stolen my story?"

He straightened his chair, stood, and went to a filing cabinet in the corner. Keeping his back to me, he pulled out a drawer and began searching. The man really was a son-of-a-bitch. I confess something I never told a soul. I admit I am a murderer. And he decides to look for something in his files.

When he came back to his desk, he was carrying a manila folder. He opened it, rifled through sheets of paper, and handed me one.

"What's that?"

"Why don't you read it?"

"I'm sorry, Doctor, but I did not come here to read about other people's problems."

"I think this will interest you."

I took the piece of paper from him and began to read. I did not have to go beyond the first few paragraphs. "How did you do this?"

"How did I do what?"

"Get my story down in my exact words while I was talking." I knew that was not what he had done, but I needed time.

"It's not your story, Mr. van Pels, or rather it is, but you're not the one who killed the man in the barn."

I was still holding the piece of paper. I dropped it on his desk.

"Why do you think you were referred to me that first time, when you lost your voice?"

"The medical doctors couldn't find anything. They said a psychiatrist was my only hope."

"Yes, but there are many psychiatrists. Why me?"

"I didn't want to drive to New York."

"I'm not the only psychiatrist in New Jersey."

This time I did not answer.

"Didn't they tell you anything else about me?"

"I don't remember."

"So you didn't know I work with survivors of the camps?"

"I have nothing in common with those people. They're frightened. They live in the past. I have put it behind me."

"You have this story in common. That paper you just read is a record of an interview in a DP camp."

"Okay, so I'm not the only guy who hacked up some Nazi bastard in a barn."

"You're probably right there. More of that sort of thing went on than we like to admit. Maybe you're one of the killers, but I don't think so. Don't ask me why. It's just a hunch."

"I didn't think psychiatrists were supposed to have hunches."

"Hunches are all we have, Mr. van Pels. But what I'm really curious about is why you're so determined to believe you're one of the murderers."

"That's the way I remember it. I even dream about it."

I waited for him to rifle through that damn folder again, and remind me that I told him I do not dream. If he did that, I was going to get up and walk out of his office. I should have already. I confess the most serious crime I ever committed, and he tells me I'm not guilty of it.

"You remember killing the German because you wanted to kill him. You and a lot of others. And when one of you did, all of you did."

"A minyan of revenge."

He tilted his head to one side quizzically, as if I had surprised him.

"You said you were not knowledgeable about your religion."

"You can't help picking things up, here and there."

■   ■   ■   ■

I KNEW as I locked the car door that I was asking for trouble. On these potholed streets, lined with crumbling buildings defaced by rage, a Cadillac was an invitation to theft.

The men were already folding their prayer shawls and unwinding their phylacteries when I arrived. I was not sorry to have missed the prayers.

The redhead came up the aisle to meet me. "Years go by, you don't come near the place. Now all of a sudden, you're a regular. You're thinking of converting back to us, maybe? It's not such a bad idea. Six million we got to replace."

"I have three children."

"Mazel tov. You're raising them Jewish?"

I shook my head no.

"I didn't think so." He slid into one of the pews and, grabbing the back of the seat in front, lowered himself to a sitting position. His jaw tightened with the effort. Chasing me up the aisle, he was fast on his feet, but bending his back was a slow exercise in agony. That was another reason I avoided people like him. I did not like to be reminded of the pain. I did not want to know what had caused it. Nonetheless, I sat beside him.

"Your wife, I bet she's not Jewish."

"She is."

He turned to me. The pale, almost invisible eyebrows arched. "This I don't get. You move heaven and earth to be a goy, then you marry a Jewish girl? You couldn't find yourself a nice shiksa?"

"I fell in love with my wife."

He lifted his eyes to the ceiling. "A romantic I got on my hands." He lowered his eyes to me. "She's the love of your life? No one else you ever looked at twice?"

"I almost married her sister." I had no idea why I was telling him this. I never thought about it anymore.

"You think this is a coincidence? All the girls give you a hard-on—you should excuse my language in shul—they just happen to be Jewish? So what happened with the sister?"

"She said she couldn't marry someone who wasn't Jewish."

"I wasn't hearing this with my own ears, I wouldn't believe it. Divine retribution, I'd say, if I believed in God, which I don't, just like you."

"You don't believe in God?"

"After what happened?"

"Then what are you doing here?"

"I already told you. Someone got to come."

"Why?"

"How many times I got to explain it to you? Cain. The minyan. The same reason you keep coming."

"I came because—" I stopped. I had no idea why I was here.

"Yes?"

I told him about the night in the barn, and what I had been believing all these years, and Gabor. His face was impassive as he listened.

"So?" he asked when I finished.

"You're not surprised?"

"What's to surprise?"

"But it's so vivid. Even in dreams."

"Dreams." He shrugged his bony shoulders. "Somebody invents a way to get rid of dreams the way they can get rid of these"—he tapped the number on his arm—"they'd make a fortune. That's what made you go to a headshrinker, you got bad dreams?"

"A little more than that." I told him about standing up at the trial, and shouting about the truth, and telling people who I was. "Nobody believed me."

"All these years you're pretending to be someone else, now nobody believes you're you, and you got your feelings hurt."

"I don't care if they believe me. But I could kill them for what they did to my father."

"Now you're a killer again."

"They've made my own wife think my father stole bread out of my mouth."

"Maybe you didn't lie so much to your wife, she wouldn't have so much trouble telling what's true from what's not."

"What makes you think I lie to my wife?"

He shot me that yellow smile. "She know you come here?"

I shook my head no.

"She know you're Jewish?"

I did not answer.

"You tell her what you told me just now, and the head-shrinker, and that court full of strangers?"

"I have to protect her. Her and my children."

"With that, I wouldn't argue. I bet you make a good life for them."

"I try."

"Nice house."

"Nice enough."

"Wall-to-wall carpeting. All the latest appliances. A deep freezer stuffed with food, I bet."

I did not answer.

"Tell me, you got a lot of mirrors in that fancy house of yours?"

So that was where he was going. "You mean how can I look myself in the mirror when I lie about being a Jew?"

"Again with the Jews. If half the people who say they are spent half as much time worrying about it as you, who say you're not, this place would be full every morning. I'm not talking about running around with a Star of David on your arm. We got enough of that from the Nazis. I'm talking about being a mensch. You know what a mensch is?"

"A man."

"A little more than that. Decent. Dependable. A stand-up guy."

"So?"

"So, I was you, I was so worried about my father's memory, I'd forget Otto Frank and go home and look in one of those mirrors in that fancy house you built to keep everyone safe."

"I believe that the worldwide acclaim given her story cannot be explained unless we recognize in it our wish to forget the gas chambers and our effort to do so by glorifying the ability to react into an extremely private, gentle, sensitive world, and there to cling as much as possible to what have been one's usual daily attitudes and activities, although surrounded by a maelstrom apt to engulf one at any moment."

— "The Ignored Lesson of Anne Frank,"
by Bruno Bettelheim, in *Anne Frank:
Reflections on Her Life and Legacy*, edited
by Hyman A. Enzer and Sandra Solotaroff-Enzer

NINETEEN

I WISH I COULD SAY that I took his advice; that I went home and told Madeleine who I was and where I had been; that I took my children on my lap and asked them what went click ninety-nine times and clack once, and when they gave up and I answered a centipede with a club foot, I explained how my father had made me laugh with that joke when I was their age. I wish I had told them that my father had a temper, but he was a good man and not a thief; that sometimes I was ashamed of my mother, what boy is not, but I loved her and would give anything not to have fought with her the night before the Green Police came; that sometimes I still blamed my father for not getting us out in time, and hated myself for getting out finally. Maybe my children would have been better off if I had told them the truth. Maybe Madeleine would have stopped threatening divorce. Or maybe it would have made no difference. Millions would still be dead, and I would still be alive. My father would still have been directed to the wrong side in the selection, or marched off months later with that group of men. I still would not be certain which it was. I still would have done nothing to stop it. But I did not tell them, and Madeleine did not leave me, and the children grew up not much happier or unhappier than other young people, as far as I could see.

We put a swimming pool in behind the house the red-haired man had taunted me about, added a sunroom to it, then sold it and moved to a bigger place that had been built before the war, with the kind of solid materials and good workmanship you couldn't get anymore. Abigail got herself arrested in an anti-war march; and Betsy walked away from the wreck of Madeleine's brand-new Volvo with nothing worse than a broken finger, thank god; and, after four years of straight A's, David almost did not graduate from the private day school he attended, because he and two friends ran through commencement exercises naked. Streaking, it was called. Compared to what happened to some of the children in the neighborhood—drugs, cults, a drunk driving accident that left two young people dead—I was lucky. Madeleine went back to school to get her master's degree in literature, took a job in the school from which David had almost been expelled, and began filling the house that was now empty of our own children with adoring, giggling girls who called themselves Ms. van Pels's gells. I think my wife was happy.

The war was ancient history, so ancient that some people were saying the Holocaust, as it was called these days, had never happened. And if the Holocaust had not happened, Anne had not written her diary. It was a hoax, the deniers insisted. Anne and Peter were not Jewish names. The paper and ink were not available in the 1940s. The writing was too good to have come from the pen of a teenage girl, the insights too perceptive, the emotions too profound. The diary was the cunning work of a Jewish-American writer named Meyer Levin, they argued. Poor Levin always had claimed he spoke in the true voice of Anne. Still I said nothing. More important people than I spoke out. Otto sued some of these new Nazis, and won, but that did not stop them. The Netherlands State Institute for War Documentation published what they called a critical edition of the diary, complete with testimony from handwriting experts and historians and scholars, but the attacks continued. What good would come from the protest of an ordinary American businessman whose name just happened by coincidence to be the same as that of a boy who had been dead for decades?

ON THE morning of August 21, 1980, I came down to find coffee perking, bread toasting, and the newspaper beside my place at the table, as usual. I sat and unfolded the *Times*. Madeleine poured my coffee. I had eaten my toast and was finishing a second cup of coffee, when I reached the obituaries.

OTTO FRANK,

FATHER OF ANNE,

DEAD AT 91

I put down my mug and sat staring at the headline beside the photo of the familiar face, gnarled now as an old tree trunk. I could not help doing the calculations. My father had died at forty-six. Younger than I was now. Given another year, Otto would have lived exactly twice my father's life. He had lived six times as long as Anne. But he had kept her memory alive. He had burnished it until it shone like a beacon, or, some were beginning to say, a klieg light blinding people to the bloodier truths of the past. Whatever he had done to my father, and Pfeffer, and the others, he had not let Anne down. I had to give him that.

I INVITED Madeleine to go with me to Amsterdam. I did want her along, no matter what she thought. But if she refused to take time off from school, which did not, after all, pay the bills, how could she expect me to drop everything at our busiest time? So I went to Amsterdam alone.

I was curious to see how the city had changed, though I had no intention of returning to 263 Prinsengracht. That was the only reason I was not sorry Madeleine had declined to come with me. She would have insisted on going to the Anne Frank Huis. That was what the building was called now. It was the city's main tourist attraction. Madeleine would not have missed it for the world.

It must have been the jet lag. I never would have got lost if I were not bleary-eyed and disoriented. True, I no longer knew the city, but I have an excellent sense of direction. Over the years, in my travels with Madeleine, I have navigated around strange cities and over unmarked country roads without losing my bearings. But I lost them that afternoon and ended up on the Prinsengracht right across from number 263.

I sat on a bench to study the small map the concierge had given me when I left the hotel. The canals lay like neat blue ribbons over the flesh-colored city. Small numbers indicated the restaurants, hotels, and nightclubs full of scantily clad women, which advertised around the margins of the map. Various symbols signified points of interest. What looked like a small Greek temple designated the Anne Frank Huis. I looked up from the map to the building across the canal. Otto's institute had done a good job of restoring it, too good. The shiny black door was freshly painted. The frames of the long windows we had not been permitted to go near for fear someone on the outside would see us were no longer rotting. Behind the house, the bare black branches of the chestnut tree knifed the winter-white sky. In my day, the tree had not shown above the house, or maybe I had simply never had the chance to see it from this vantage point. I put the map back in my pocket, stood, and made my way across the canal. I was not lost, of course. I had passed half a dozen signs pointing the way.

How can I describe walking through the house? My past was everywhere, and nowhere. It stuck like grit between the floorboards, worn smooth by how many millions of feet. It glared down at me from the map where we had followed the progress of the Allies, who arrived too late for my mother and father and Anne and Margot and Mrs. Frank and Pfeffer. It winked at me from the gauzy curtains painted with faint figures to make it look as if the Green Police were marching Jews to their death on the street beneath the windows. Clever touch, that. It crouched upstairs where I had flung my mother around in a jitterbug of love and fury that had thrown us both off balance. It seethed in the suffocating coffin of a bedroom where I had lain, my stomach flexing its hunger like a muscle, my mind racing with plots of revenge against the man who had sent me to bed without supper, who had let us end up like this. It was all there, but smaller, of course, seen through the wrong end of a telescope. It was all accurate, the pictures of movie stars and royalty over the place where Anne's bed had stood, the kettle on the stove, the dish towel hanging beside the sink. Otto had had plenty of time to see to everything before he died. And it was all wrong. It was wrong the way my memories all these years, even when I misremembered, had been right. In place of the silence we had observed was the shuffle of shoes made in a dozen different countries, and the murmurs of excuse me and thank you in several different languages, and the respectful whispers of awe and dismay. But these people did not know what a whisper was, because they could not conceive the damage an inadvertent sound could do. Instead of the rank stench of human fear, there was the insipid smell of human sweat. Evil was no more than a sleight of hand etched on a window shade. Everything was cleverly planned and expertly wrought, but nothing was true. Nothing was as bad as it was inside my head.

I came out of the house and stood for a moment with my back to it, getting my bearings. An ash gray dusk was falling on the city. I had forgotten how early darkness comes to Amsterdam in the winter. A cold wind skimmed across the greasy black canal. The last tourists streamed past me, their masks of solemnity cracking in the fresh air, their voices rising in giddy relief at their escape.

I turned left and started back along the Prinsengracht. As I

came around the corner in front of the Westerkerk, the bells
began to chime. In the annex, the sound had been deafening,
until they melted down the bells, and the silence had been
worse, but here on the street, the reverberation barely troubled
the air. The herring seller was closing up his stand, but the
flower vendor and the newspaper and tobacco kiosk were still
doing a lively business. Bicyclists pedaled home with briefcases
and groceries and children stuffed into wooden crates fastened
to the handlebars or strapped above the rear wheel. The army
of cyclists was better dressed than I remembered, and there
were more women among them. In the old days, the women
would have been home preparing supper.

I must have been ten or eleven. Ten, I think, because it is an
early summer evening, and I will turn eleven in the fall. My
father and I are on our way back to the flat where my mother is
still unpacking the few possessions we managed to bring with
us from Osnabrück. My father is full of optimism. He has left
at the border the fear and indecision that made him snap at me
on the train. He is Dutch by birth; this is a homecoming. We
have left Germany and its insane new order behind. The
Germans will come to their senses someday. In the meantime, we
will be better off in Amsterdam. We will be safe in Amsterdam.
In the last war, the Netherlands remained neutral.

As my father and I stand waiting for the light to change, he
pats first one pocket, then the next, looking for his cigarettes.
"One minute," he tells me as he starts for the stand. I follow
him, hoping for candy, knowing the impossibility of the hope.
We are on our way home to supper.

Standing in front of the stall, my father takes the pack of
cigarettes from the vendor, tears it open, puts one between his

lips, and holds a match to it. Only then does he take his change from the small metal tray. He is about to drop the coins in his pocket, when he seems to think better of it and draws his hand, still holding the coins, out again. My hopes soar. He moves on to the flower stall.

"What do you think, Peter, lilies or tulips?" He does not suggest carnations. Those are for my mother's birthday, year after year. This occasion is unique. He does not mention roses either. They are beyond our pocketbook. Though things will be all right as soon as he gets on his feet again, wriggling out of the hands of the Nazis was not cheap. But who needs roses, with lilies gleaming in the twilight and tulips burning like flames?

When we start to walk on, his chin is higher and his back straighter. He reaches up and readjusts his hat at a jaunty angle. He is a man again, the man I have not seen for some time. I can barely keep pace with his long swaggering stride. I have forgotten the candy. I am forgetting the boys in the schoolyard who called me Christ-killer. I am trying to keep up with my father, who is hurrying through the rosy Amsterdam evening toward my mother, who will open the door of the freshly scrubbed, supper-smelling flat to find her husband and son standing there, a bunch of scarlet tulips burning between them.

A man collided into my back, excused himself, and moved on, but I was suddenly aware of other passersby. They looked at me, then quickly away, embarrassed but not surprised. We are a stone's throw from the Anne Frank House. Weeping tourists are not a rarity. But I was not crying for anything in that house. I was crying for the innocence of that father walking home through the blushing Amsterdam evening, for the hope of that woman scrubbing a new flat for a new life, for the boy who thought he was safe. I was crying for a world that saw a war coming, that feared the worst, but had no inkling how bad the worst could be. I was crying for a world that, for all its misery, had not heard of concentration camps, or mass showers that spray death, or chimneys that spew human ashes, or medical experiments on men who happen to have red hair or children who happen to be twins. I was crying for a paradise I had tried to recreate for my wife and children, and myself, and for my failure. As the silent tears gave way to sobs, and people turned to stare, because this was more than they were accustomed to, I cried for the second murder of my parents, the one I had committed by silence.

IT IS a funny thing, the various ways in which people react to being fooled. Some take it personally, though my wife, the only one, other than my children, who had a right to, did not. She knew the lies had nothing to do with her. Her reaction was relief. She had always suspected something. It was reassuring, she said, to know that what I was hiding was not worse. I did not ask her what she meant by that. I had a better idea than she of the crimes I could have committed.

My children did not blame me either. Unlike their mother, however, they could not imagine why I had kept silent all these years. Perhaps I had not failed to protect them after all.

The children took to their new past with a vengeance. Abigail had her first child, my first grandchild, that spring, and named him Herman, spelled with one *n* and shortened to Hank. Two years after that, she called her daughter Augusta, after my mother. I was surprised, and pleased. Four later, Betsy named her first son Peter. She had not changed her name when she married—I could not understand that, but she pointed out that her medical degree was in the name of van Pels, and since her husband did not complain, it was not my place to—so the boy was Peter van Pels-Gallagher. It was, as the customs officer had said so many years ago, a good American name.

My partner, Harry, was delighted. He had never been able to understand how we got on so well. My being Jewish restored his faith in an orderly universe.

Others' reactions were more muted. I do not mean to imply that I went around making announcements to the world, but somehow word traveled. Or perhaps I only imagined it did. Perhaps I saw a difference in people's eyes and detected it in their manner because I expected to. This habit of dividing the world into two camps does not die easily. Certainly, George Johnson continued to treat me with the same bluff professional friendliness.

The one who took the news hardest was my sister-in-law Susannah. She could not forgive my cosmic sin. As I had learned years ago, she might not be able to love a gentile, but she could only hate a Jew who tried to pass, or, as her husband, who was equally critical though not so vocal, put it, "buy white." She accused me of being a self-hating Jew. She charged me with being a secret anti-Semite. She sounded like Meyer Levin ranting at Otto Frank, though it occurs to me now that Otto had been more comfortable in his lightweight Jewish clothing than poor Levin ever was in his thin Jewish skin.

Madeleine defended me to her sister. The quarrel was so dire they did not telephone each other for ten days, which in that family was a record. Madeleine insisted that Susannah was just angry because if I had told the truth thirty-three years earlier, she, rather than Madeleine, would be married to me. The argument was flattering, but unconvincing. Susannah was happy with Norman. And she must have known there were times when her sister had been miserable with me. But perhaps my wife is on to something. Is the notion that Susannah might be carrying a torch for me any more ludicrous than that she found God in six million shrouds? Is the likelihood of her bearing a grudge against me any more far-fetched than that of her shouldering suffering she never experienced by people she had felt no connection to until they were gone? I do not resent her espousal of the faith, only her vicarious wearing of the yellow star. But I did not say any of that to her. She was Madeleine's sister, and unlike the rest of my wife's family who quarrel and reconcile so cavalierly, I know there is not always enough time to make amends.

"Isn't there something we must do to pay for being alive?"

—Meyer Levin, quoted in *The Stolen Legacy of Anne Frank: Meyer Levin, Lillian Hellman, and the Staging of the Diary*, by Ralph Melnick

EPILOGUE

Amsterdam, 2003

THIS TIME MADELEINE WAS WITH ME. I had hoped to bring the whole family, that was why I had scheduled the trip for the summer, but my children have lives of their own. Even the grandchildren have lives of their own. The younger ones go to camps to play tennis and act in plays and, in the case of Abigail's youngest, Amanda, lose weight. I cannot understand a summer camp, an extremely expensive summer camp, dedicated to hunger, but I know enough to keep my mouth shut. The older go on student tours or travel with friends. So Madeleine and I came to Amsterdam alone, and on the first afternoon she walked through the house at 263 Prinsengracht by my side. Afterward, we sat on a bench across the canal.

The chestnut tree had grown closer to the sky since my last visit. Dusty brown leaves clung to the branches, though it was only the end of August. A punishing heat wave had baked western Europe dry as clay, and a human scandal was sweeping France in its wake. Unwilling to forfeit their summer holidays, families left aging immobile parents alone in Paris. Headlines screamed of old people expiring in oven-hot flats, while their children and grandchildren cavorted on Mediterranean beaches and splashed in alpine lakes. I felt sorry for those old people, who were probably no older than I, but I worried about their children. They had no idea what was in store for them.

It was past five, but the sun puddled in pools of gold on the surface of the canals, which, according to the guidebook, were cleaner than they had been in years. The entire city was sanitizing itself. Prostitutes stayed in their windows, or at least in the designated quarter. You could go for whole blocks without being accosted by someone eager to sell you drugs. "It's getting more like it used to be," the concierge had said to me that morning. He was too young to know how it used to be, and I did not tell him. I have confessed to my wife and children, her family and my partner, but I see no reason to confide in strangers. These days Holocaust victims, as we are called, are celebrities du jour. I read that in a magazine after the movie *Schindler's List* came out. Some of us, though I am not among them, have our names on identification cards, which visitors to the museum in Washington, D.C., pick up on their way into the exhibit. I know because my grandson Peter brought one back for me when he visited. I had expected something like my Certificate of Identity in Lieu of a Passport, but my Certificate had listed only the bare facts, not even my religion. This card told a story. "So-and-so was the only child of Jewish parents . . . his father worked as a salesman . . . until the war the Jewish community was the third largest in Germany . . . he went to a Catholic boys' school . . . he emigrated to the United States in . . ." The boy in Peter's card had lived, but many of the cards, most of the cards, recounted tales of the dead. On the inside of the front cover there was a peculiar sentence. "This card tells the story of a real person who lived during the Holocaust." Why should they have to say that?

Do not misunderstand me. I am in favor of the museum, though I will not visit it. Someone must make sure that children learn what happened, and adults remember, and students study, and scholars try to make sense of the senseless. My son David, who teaches history at a college in New England, frequently uses the archives. But something about the identity card that tourists pick up on their way into the museum and discard in a trash can on a District of Columbia sidewalk on their way out offends me. Even if they keep the card as a memento of their visit, it offends me. It is playacting. It is like my sentimental sister-in-law who claims victimization by proxy.

Beside me on the bench, Madeleine asked if I was ready to start back to the hotel. I said I was, and we helped each other up. As we made our way across the bridge over the canal and onto the plaza in front of the church, the Westerkerk bells stirred the hot air. We were passing the statue now. I was not going to look at it.

It is not even a decent likeness. It is a bad imitation of a Degas ballerina. Even Madeleine, who does not know what she looked like, except from photographs in books and magazines, and on silk scarves sold as souvenirs, and the side of a medieval tower in England where Jews were massacred in the Middle Ages, has pronounced the statue kitsch. I do not want to look at it, but as we make our way past, my head swivels. Then I realize it is not the statue that has caught my attention, but the flurry of motion around it.

A little girl, perhaps eight or nine, younger than Anne, but bigger—this child has not been starved; this child has grown up on pizza and ice cream and Big Macs, though she does not look American—stands beside the statue, her fingers clasping Anne's bronze hand, her blond ponytails resting against Anne's head, her smile shy but proud.

"Lächeln," a man's voice behind me shouts, though if the child were smiling any wider, her face would crack.

"Lächeln," a woman's voice echoes.

I turn and see a couple, the father's expression half hidden behind a digital camera, the mother grinning almost as broadly as her daughter.

"Smile," they shout again, as their heads come together to see the digitalized image of their daughter hanging on the bronze statue of a little Jewish girl.

Madeleine takes my arm and begins walking. My temper has softened with age and cooled since my confession. I no longer fly off the handle for no reason. But still she does not trust me, especially in a situation like this. "It's only a statue," she says, as she tries to lead me away.

She is right, of course. It is only a statue of Anne, a tribute, supposedly. It is less than the real thing, and, in its ability to summon and bowdlerize memory, more.

I let Madeleine lead me away, but I cannot help turning back every few steps to watch the family recording the happiness of their holiday. It is not their fault. The couple look young, younger than my own children. Their parents probably were not born when I went into hiding. The child is only a child. But I cannot help myself. I recognize the irony of what I am about to say, the absurdity of it. Who is at fault here, the German family or me? But there is enough blame to go around.

As I move off, I say in a voice loud enough for the German with the camera and his ignorant wife and their unknowing child to hear; shrill enough for the proprietors of the stalls, and the people buying flowers on their way home, and even some of the cyclists waiting for the light to change to turn their heads; fierce enough to set up a tremor in my own chest.

"My God, have they no memory?"

ACKNOWLEDGMENTS

IN THE WINTER OF 1994, on a tour of the Anne Frank House, my imagination was captured by a guide's remark that records exist documenting the fate of all the inhabitants of the secret annex except Peter van Daan, as she called him, in keeping with the names Anne Frank used in her diary. If this young man did not die with the others, I speculated, what might he have gone on to? When I began the research for this book, I discovered that the guide was either misinformed or romantically inclined. According to Netherlands Red Cross dossier 135177, Peter perished in Mauthausen concentration camp on

May 5, 1945, three days before it was liberated. By the time I'd discovered this, however, Peter van Pels had been living in my mind for several years.

This novel is the result of the life Peter took on. It is based on what we know about him, his family, Fritz Pfeffer, and the other inhabitants of the secret annex, as well as the facts about the subsequent history of the diary, the movie and play made from it, and the lawsuits surrounding it in this country and abroad. I have, of course, imagined the letters sent to Peter by Otto Frank's attorneys and Meyer Levin.

For help in researching the story, I am grateful to the Anne Frank Stichting in Amsterdam, the Anne Frank-Fonds in Basel, the Wisconsin State Historical Society, the Boston University Special Collections, the United States Holocaust Memorial Museum, the New York Public Library for the Performing Arts, the Dorot Jewish Division of the New York Public Library, and the entire staff of the New York Society Library. Among the scores of people who were generous with their time, expertise, and memories, I am especially indebted to Liza Bennett, Greg Gallagher, Nancy Hathaway, Nimet Habachy, Joan Leiman, Ralph Melnick, Arthur Rosenblatt, Fred Smoler, Michael Schwartz, Sharon Stein, and Marie Stoess. I also want to thank Richard Snow and Fred Allen, superb editors and good friends, who took time off from their work to read and comment on mine. And I am once again especially grateful to my editor Starling Lawrence for goading me on, reining me in, and executing both tasks with kindness and wit; my agent Emma Sweeney for her unflagging support and profound and thought-provoking insights; and my husband, Stephen Reibel, who introduced me to Peter.